Praise for Mina Carter's *Perfect Mate*

"The love scenes are scorching in their intensity. This is a novel that is truly a treat to read, and one that readers will adore as much as I have."

~ *Night Owl Reviews*

"I truly fell in love with the story line and characters in *Perfect Mate*. It was so action-packed though, that I didn't stop to take a breath for probably three-fourths of the book... I definitely recommend *Perfect Mate* to anyone who loves paranormal books with an amazing group of characters and a uniquely written plot."

~ *Sizzling Hot Book Reviews*

"Mina Carter has created wonderful characters and a fascinating storyline; the book will keep you enraptured from the first moment. There are many torrid, romantic, and funny scenes and with every single one, you will slip deeper under its magic."

~ *Confessions from Romaholics*

Look for these titles by

Mina Carter

Now Available:

Reaper

Perfect Mate

Solar Storm

Print Anthology

End of Days

Perfect Mate

Mina Carter

SAMHAIN
PUBLISHING

Samhain Publishing, Ltd.
11821 Mason Montgomery Road, 4B
Cincinnati, OH 45249
www.samhainpublishing.com

Perfect Mate

Print ISBN: 978-1-61921-277-0
Digital ISBN: 978-1-60928-867-9

Editing by Amy Sherwood
Cover by Kanaxa

First Samhain Publishing, Ltd. electronic publication: August 2012
First Samhain Publishing, Ltd. print publication: July 2013

Dedication

To Milly, for being prepared to help me bury bodies in the backyard. To Will and BJ, for always being there. To Amy, for not running away screaming at a story littered with Britspeak.

And a special mention for all those readers who have stuck with me since the beginning, and those just taking a chance now. Thank you from the bottom of my heart.

Chapter One

She dreamed of the forest and running. Of the wind as she raced over the terrain. Her footing steady and sure...she was agile, fleet-footed and free. The sounds and smells of nature filled her senses, earthy and comforting, as she slowed her pace.

The darkness of night surrounded her, with only the silvery moon lighting her way as she padded on silent feet through the mountain forest trails. Despite the fact she was alone, she didn't feel threatened out here in the dark. Instead, she felt comforted, as though nature itself would rise and protect her if danger should strike.

The sound of a stream up ahead drew her attention, so she turned toward it. As she approached, the musical notes of it rushing and tumbling over mountain stones grew louder.

She could already feel the cold, crystal-clear water against her tongue as she reached the bank, dropping her head to drink and coming face to face with the reflection of amber-gold eyes—

"Lillian...Lilly! Wake up, chick. We got incoming!"

The sound of the ward sister Beth's voice snapped Lillian Rosewood out of her light doze. On reflex, she stood up, smoothing down her plain shirt and slacks before fully awake. As the manager at St. Mary's, most of the staff were aware of her dedication to the hospital her great-grandfather had founded. The sight of her asleep at her desk or on the small sofa in her office rather than going home wasn't an uncommon one.

"Incoming?"

She rushed out of the room in a heartbeat, following the bustling senior nurse as she hurried down to the reception area. "What do you mean incoming? It's after eleven...there's been no phone call..."

She slid to a halt just inside the medical reception area, almost running Beth over as the nurse came to an abrupt stop in front of her. The area beyond the other woman had become a hive of activity. Army medics burst through the double doors, shoving a gurney between them, accompanied by a blast of cold wind from the wintry weather outside.

"Crap."

Even from here she could see the blood. It covered the torso and legs of the patient on the gurney, vivid scarlet against the subdued greens of his combat uniform. Her brow furrowed. Where were the dressings? There was nothing, not even a swab of gauze held over the bloodstained fabric.

"What are you doing?"

She brushed past Beth, a frown creasing her brow and authority ringing in her voice. "You can't bring him in here like that. This is a psychiatric institution. We don't provide emergency care."

Even as she tried to stop them, her heart went out to the soldier on the bed. Tall, he had to be well over six feet, and from the bits she could see that weren't covered in blood, ripped too. Irritation surged through her. What kind of sicko noticed how cute the patient was while said patient bled out in the lobby?

"For Christ's sake, someone put pressure on that wound."

She surged forward, even though she didn't have protective

gloves on, her instincts overriding any sense of personal danger. Before she could reach the sodden fabric, a hand clamped over her wrist. The coppery, tangy scent of blood rolled over her, surrounding her and trying to trigger her gag reflex. Instincts as old as humanity itself told her that something was wrong. She'd never seen so much blood on a patient who didn't become a corpse.

"Don't."

Bright amber eyes glared out of a pain-ravaged face. Gasping, she tried to step back, but his hold was like iron around her slender wrist. A manacle of flesh and blood. No one should move that quickly, especially not someone as injured as him.

Within a heartbeat, the tension among the military medics surrounding them went up a couple of notches. As though they expected the guy on the bed to leap off it and attack her. She shook her head at such silliness. Call themselves medics? Anyone with the slightest bit of medical training could see that this guy wasn't going anywhere fast.

She didn't fight his hold in case she hurt him more. The wheels of the gurney squeaked as he pulled her closer.

"Don't move," she warned, looking down for the nametag on his chest. *Capt. J. Harper.* She couldn't help wondering what the J stood for. "I'm Lilly. It's okay, I can help. Just stay still for me, okay?"

She kept her voice deliberately low and soft, pitched to reassure and relax. She'd worked at St. Mary's since she left college, and a person couldn't work in a psychiatric hospital for all that time without learning a thing or two about dealing with patients. Especially patients twice her weight who could snap her like a twig with ease. Unbidden, a shiver of excitement wormed its way through her veins. He was a soldier...the take-charge sort of guy who inhabited her fantasies.

A flush of heat hit her cheeks as shame washed over her. She couldn't...no, she *wouldn't*...fantasize over a badly injured soldier in her care, no matter how good looking he was. It was wrong, just wrong.

"You can't help me," he rasped as his eyes bored into hers.

They were an unusual color. Not the amber she'd thought, but a burnished, deep gold. They pleaded with her, as though begging for something...but she didn't know what. Still with her wrist caught in his bigger, strong hand, he searched her eyes in desperation, as though looking for something.

Something he didn't find. His lip curling in disgust, he thrust her hand away and turned his head.

"Go away. No one can help me."

She was the one. Even in the depths of his drug-induced madness Jack could still feel the presence of the woman from the reception area earlier. He'd caught her scent, drawn it into his sensitive nose and down into his lungs, making it a part of him. The beast inside had unraveled, lifting its head and taking notice at the first whiff of faded perfume mixed with strawberry shampoo and the musk of pure woman.

In a heartbeat, it had decided she belonged to them and memorized her scent. Now, wherever she went, no matter how far and fast she tried to run, the beast inside him would be able to find her. If he got out of here before they killed him, at least.

The silver nitrate they'd given him raged through his body, dulling his senses and locking his abilities down tighter than an inmate in Alcatraz. The beast inside, the creature they'd created in a lab and spliced to his genetic code, raged against its confinement. Raged against the cage of DNA, flesh and bone the silver had locked it into. It didn't matter. Even stuck in his human form, he could feel her.

Struggling, he fought against his bonds again. It was futile. In his weakened state he wouldn't have been able to fight his way out of a paper bag, much less the high-tensile restraints on the gurney. He needed the strength of the beast they'd given him to escape their clutches. Something he'd been so close to doing before they'd figured out his plans.

Before he knew it, it had been ordnance and explosives in the barrack and armed commandos putting enough lead in him to drop a rhino. He planned to get some payback for that.

"Put him in there. Give him another dose and leave him to calm down," a doctor announced. He'd heard enough of them in his time with the Project to recognize one when he heard him. This one sounded pissed.

"Just what the fuck where you thinking...letting that woman near him? She could have touched him—"

Jack's mind went off on a tangent, easily distracted by the memory of a soft voice and sexy-as-hell scent. *God, yeah.* She could have touched him. He'd wanted her to touch him. He'd *ached* for her to touch him.

If she had, or if he'd contacted her skin instead of grabbing her sleeve-covered wrist, nothing would have stopped him claiming her there and then. Not even the torn skin and shredded muscles where his abs used to be. Just the touch of her skin, the skin of his destined mate, would have sealed the bond between them and released the creature inside him.

"She didn't."

He tuned out the familiar whine as his guards tried to justify themselves. He'd heard it all before. His two jailers weren't that inventive, so it was the same old tried and tested excuses of the government-funded, under-qualified drone.

The argument raged on as they pushed his gurney into a

room. It came to a stop under a window. He sighed in relief as he looked up at the cloudy night sky. Something in his soul eased at the tenuous link with nature. He was what he was, what they'd made him into... A creature of the wilds. A creature of the forest and the mountains.

Not a man. Never a man. Not anymore.

Four hours, twenty-three minutes and...oh yes, six seconds.

Lillian looked at the clock on the wall of her office and sighed. She'd never been any good at resisting temptation. A fact so well known that the nurses had gotten her a T-shirt made with the words *I can resist anything but temptation* emblazoned across the front for Christmas last year.

Right now, Captain Harper was her temptation. There had been something about the soldier that caught her attention. Quite what, she didn't know. For one, she was far too old for him. Mid-thirties and a guy who couldn't be more than mid-twenties? It made her feel a little too cougarish for Lillian's comfort.

Those eyes, though. There had been something about them. Something that reached inside her and pulled at her heartstrings. She snorted. *Pulled? Hell, the way they'd been twanging, he could have played a whole concerto on them.* Admitting defeat, she pushed her chair back and left her office. She wouldn't be able to settle until she'd checked on him.

It took less than five minutes to reach the restricted ward. She still didn't know why they'd brought him here, other than some excuse about it being the nearest facility, but he'd been injured. Since the hospital housed psychiatric patients rather than medical emergencies, it was her duty to ensure he was okay.

Yeah, you just keep telling yourself that.

Used to seeing her in the corridors, the two soldiers on guard duty eyed her with boredom as she passed in front of them, intending to loop back through the empty wards beyond. Her heels clicked on the stone tiles as she walked. She loved the history of this place, loved the feeling that she followed in the footsteps of previous hospital staff as she went about her rounds.

The military wing seemed mostly deserted. Unlike the rest of the patients, none of the soldiers were long-term residents. They arrived, were seen by the military doctors and were transferred out again. Sometimes in the same night.

Despite her curiosity, it was something she'd gotten used to. All her questions had fallen on deaf ears, even when she'd petitioned her grandfather, the current owner of St. Mary's. Every time she asked, she got the same reply. The Army leased the south wing, and they paid an exorbitant sum to do so. They brought their own staff in, all medically trained and occupationally competent. When they were on site, the south wing was, to all intents and purposes, no longer part of the hospital.

She stopped outside the last room—Harper's room—and grimaced as she realized how cell-like it appeared. St. Mary's was an old hospital, built in the days when mental illnesses were commonly treated with containment, and restraint—among other, more brutal methods—was commonplace. She shivered. Thankfully the north wing, where treatments were carried out in those days, had long since been demolished and replaced with a serene garden.

The metal door stood slightly ajar, which alleviated the cell-like impression a little, but not enough for her liking. Beyond it, she could see the motionless figure strapped to the bed. Her jaw dropped in shock. Despite the fact he'd been badly injured, they still had him in restraints? What kind of animals were they…how on Earth could this be good for a patient's mental health or recovery?

"Captain Harper?"

Her whisper seemed so loud, more like a shout, as she edged into the room. The thrill of the forbidden shot through her. She couldn't be caught down here, not in a patient's room. Hospital staff weren't allowed in this area, on pain of dismissal. But it would be kind of hard to sack the owner's granddaughter, a fact she reassured herself with as she padded forward.

"Captain Harper? I came to see how you're doing. Do you feel any better?"

She crept nearer to the bed, her eyes wide in the semi darkness. The room had been scrubbed down recently. She could smell the medical grade antibacterial cleanser she'd ordered a couple of weeks ago. Pine fresh. Yummy.

They'd changed his clothes, at least. Instead of the torn and bloodstained uniform he'd arrived in, he now wore one of the ubiquitous, backless hospital gowns. The ones where the patient's ass hung out for all to see. Normally that bugged the shit out of her. People came into hospital to get better, not to be further stripped of dignity. Creases formed between her brows as her gaze skimmed over his flat stomach. The fabric lay against his skin, and she could see the vague outline of his hip. It didn't look like they'd even bothered to put any dressings over his abdominal wounds.

Concern shot through her. He'd been gut-shot and bleeding heavily when they'd brought him. The sorts of wounds that earned a man a couple of weeks on his back with his guts taped back in as his skin healed. That is, if he survived. Most didn't.

They should have cleaned him up, redressed his wounds and settled him with his legs elevated to keep the pressure off his abdomen. Without dressings, the slightest movement would tear the wounds open again, and he'd bleed out...

Her face paled in a heartbeat, leaving her feeling shaky. Had he passed away already? That would explain the lack of dressings. Oh God, she was looking at a corpse... No, he couldn't be dead. At least, his chest rose and fell, and the breath she'd been holding punched out of her lungs.

"What the...?"

Her words stilled on her lips as she reached the bed and looked down at the man lying motionless on it. There were no wounds, leaking or otherwise. In fact, he looked perfectly healthy, as though he'd walked in off the street and decided to have a quick nap rather than be at death's door. His eyes snapped open at the sound of her voice. She was locked in place by a pair of piercing blue eyes. Her breath stuttered.

His eyes had been amber before.

Contacts, the rational part of her brain supplied. The medical staff must have removed them when they'd cleaned him up.

A broad smile curved his lips at the sight of her, and her breathing caught for entirely different reasons. He was gorgeous. Absolutely sex-on-a-stick gorgeous. The kind of looks that should be gracing the center spread in the glossy magazines Beth favored, his high cheekbones and pouting lips somehow managed to be wholly masculine.

"Lilly, Lilly, give me your answer do..."

Whatever Lillian had expected, it wasn't for him to break into song. Panic flared through her.

"Shsssh, shhhh. Be quiet."

She flapped her hands to try and enforce the need for silence as she cast an anxious glance at the door. The noise he was making, someone had to have heard him.

"*Please,* be quiet," she begged as he launched into the next line with gusto.

"...I'm half crazy, all for the love of you."

She slapped her hand over his mouth. To her relief he stopped singing. Instead, he licked her palm. The warm, wet brush of his tongue startled her and made her snatch her hand back.

"Ewww. What is *wrong* with you?" Her skin tingled where he'd licked her, and she felt the warm brush all the way down to her toes. But he...he'd *licked* her. That was *not* normal behavior.

"He's a total fucking fruit loop. That's what's wrong with him."

Chapter Two

Jack almost blew his cover at the sound of the new voice in the room. Not that it could be described as a cover. It really was him, Jack Harper, signed into the mental hospital, rather than some fancy cover identity. Really was him they were pumping full of the drugs his extensive medical records told them were necessary to keep him pliable.

Rather than the ravening monster he knew he was.

Unfortunately for them, Jack had been canny. For the last year, he and the majority of his squad had toed the line. They ate what they were told to, slept when they were told and pissed on command like good little lab rats. Not a single one of them had displayed any of the abilities the project scientists didn't know they had.

All that careful planning and subterfuge added up to one thing. They needed a shit-load more drugs than they were currently using to keep him immobile. He'd already burned through half of what they'd pumped into him just after he'd arrived. Scared that he'd almost managed physical contact with a female, they'd shot him up with enough silver to plate a tank.

It made absolutely no difference. His beast had her scent, and it wanted her. All it would take is for the moon to break through the clouds it played peek-a-boo behind. Then the blessed kiss of lunar rays would burn the rest of the crap out of his system in a heartbeat.

"Fruit loop! Fruit loop!" he agreed cheerily, playing up the madness angle as he tried to work loose the wrist hidden from view. The manacle was steel, not laced with silver, but in his weakened state and with his wolf out of reach, he couldn't break through it as easily as he normally would.

Come on. Just one blast of moonlight and he'd be good to go. Already he could feel the silver nitrate under his skin. It was so close to the surface that a light sweat would push it through his pores. Some religious cults talked about sweating blood—Jack would sweat silver. Perhaps he'd start a new trend.

"What we have here is a one hundred-percent, bonafide nut case."

The doctor's voice accompanied his footsteps as he came farther into the room. The woman by Jack's side shrank away. It was a small gesture, one he figured she wasn't aware of. Within a second, she straightened up as if she realized that she shouldn't project fear. *Interesting.* She seemed more afraid of the doctor than a possible homicidal maniac.

"He's a total loss. Post-traumatic stress disorder, completely unhinged. There's nothing we can do for him here. We'll ship him out in the morning to someplace with padded walls and hose-down surfaces, so he can talk nonsense and piss himself in peace."

Jack suppressed a snort. That was Project speak for driving him out someplace private to put a bullet in the back of his head while the silver had him locked down. He and others like him could heal most things, but even they would struggle with a wound inflicted at point-blank range.

"What are you doing in here, Lillian? You know this area is out of bounds to all non-military personnel."

The doc's voice changed tone, and even in this form Jack

could smell fear rolling off the woman. He had a first name to go with the "L. Rosewood" on her nametag. Yes, that was right, but she'd called herself Lilly in the lobby. Damn them and their injections. He'd lost part of his first memory of her. Instead, the beast snarled, its anger with the Project and the men who ran it increasing another notch.

Lillian.

He rolled the name around in his head as the doc approached. She edged around the bed a little more. Jack's protective instincts flared. He didn't care that he was pumped full of silver nitrate and strapped to the bed. If this asshole put a hand on her, Jack would take it off at the wrist. Perhaps even the shoulder. Yeah, the shoulder sounded like a good place to start...

"I needed something from one of the stores cupboards at the end of the corridor. Didn't see the point in filling out seventeen forms, in triplicate, for a couple of dressings, so I used the back corridor."

The doc made a small sound of surprise. Obviously he hadn't known of another way onto the ward. Interesting. His little rose knew the layout of the place better than the military personnel.

"Then you were a bad girl, Lillian. Do you know what happens to bad girls?"

Jack didn't need an expanded sense of smell to pick up the lust rolling off the guy. It oozed from his pores thickly, filling the room as much as it filled his voice. Feeling sick, Jack stopped breathing through his nose, but he could do nothing to block his ears. *Come on...can't the guy pick a better line to use for intimidation?*

"They get told about their behavior, a note entered on their permanent record and let off with a warning?"

He wanted to applaud. Lillian's voice was firm and no nonsense, without a hint of the fear he could smell on her skin as she edged around the bed away from the doctor stalking her.

He barked a laugh. "Very funny Lillian. I always did like that about you, you have a great sense of humor. Right now, though, I have other plans for that pretty little mouth of yours."

"Okay, enough's enough, Dr. Walker. I apologize for the transgression but—let me out." Her voice grew sharper, and a fresh wave of fear rolled from her as the doctor blocked her escape. "My grandfather will hear of this."

Walker snorted. "Yeah, right. Like you think I'm bothered about your grandfather? Sweetpea, you tell anyone and there won't be a place you can run that I won't find you. Understand?"

A growl started at the back of Jack's throat. Low and full of menace, it hovered just on the edge of human hearing. He knew they wouldn't hear it, not consciously. The tension in the room rose sharply. The human was dead. Deader than dead. He wasn't even going to be a corpse when Jack was done with him...just a red smear on the floor.

He watched as Lillian tried to slip around the edge of the bed.

"Oh, no you don't."

Grabbing the edge of the gurney, the doctor rammed it up against the wall, and cut off her escape. Jack closed his eyes as the growl got louder. A woman was about to be raped in front of him.

Not on his watch.

Reaching deep inside, he called to the part of himself that wasn't human. The part the military scientists had awoken after they'd persuaded him to "volunteer" for their enhancement tests.

"Nowhere left to run, Lillian. Now be a good girl. This won't hurt."

There was a scuffle. She screamed. A sound quickly cut off. Fury flared through him at the terrified whimpering that followed. He couldn't see what was going on, but he could imagine it. Imagine how the human had her pinned in the corner, his hand over her mouth. Rage flowed through his body like a surfer at the crest of a wave. It galvanized his limbs, eating away at the silver that kept him more a prisoner than the restraints on his wrists and ankles.

"That's it, baby. Just relax. You'll enjoy it."

The sound of sloppy kisses and whimpering filled his ears. Opening his eyes, he looked up through the window above the bed. *Clear, you bastards, clear,* he screamed silently at the clouds over the moon. He hadn't asked for what they'd done to him, and he'd never complained. The least the bitch-fates could do was allow the disaster of his life to benefit at least one person.

He held his breath as, above him, the clouds parted. Moonlight streamed through the gap, cascading through the window and spilling over his prone body. Relief and strength flooded his system in equal amounts, slamming into his starved muscles. Hot on its heels flowed in the pain. White-hot pain that stole his breath as his energized body rejected the nitrate in his blood. He gritted his teeth as silver sweat beaded on his skin.

With a roar, he ripped the manacles from his wrists and ankles. The bed slammed into the opposite wall with a metallic squeal of protest as he launched himself from it.

Oh God. Lillian couldn't believe what was happening. All she'd wanted was to check on a patient. Alleviate her concern.

Not get pinned to a wall, being groped and pawed at as Dr. Walker tried to shove his tongue down her throat.

She knew Walker fancied her. He'd asked her out shortly after being transferred to the hospital with the military unit. Just the thought of him touching her with his cold, clammy hands had made her skin crawl so, politely, she'd let him down. Obviously he hadn't taken that rejection quite as well as she'd thought.

Bile rose in her throat, her stomach rolled. She couldn't believe he was doing this. Everyone, even the military staff, knew she was the old man's granddaughter.

Whimpering in not-so-mock fear, she allowed him to pull her closer. He shoved his groin—and the thick erection—forward and ground it roughly against her. At the feeling of the hard ridge pressing into her soft belly, she almost lost it and kneed him in the balls. She held off. He was at the wrong angle for her knee to connect properly. She'd only get one shot, so it had to be right.

"Baby, you feel so good. I knew you'd be good."

He planted sloppy kisses all over her cheeks and latched onto her mouth again with the rubbery fish lips she'd shuddered over with the other female staff. She gritted her teeth as he tried to force her lips open. *So not happening.* She'd bite his tongue off first, perhaps right after she planted her knee into his groin.

Just a little more, she begged silently as he shifted position against her. *Just a little more and he'll be in the right position.*

Before she could put her big plan into action, the room flooded with moonlight and a full-throated snarl erupted behind Walker. Her heart thundered so loud she thought momentarily she'd imagined the growl. Opening her mouth, she prepared to bite Walker's lip as she slammed her knee into his family jewels, but she never got the chance. The next instant the doctor was ripped away from her and slammed into the opposite wall.

Her chest heaved as adrenalin and surprise thundered through her. Her heart battering against her ribcage, she looked up, expecting to see one of the guards or maybe even a couple of the male orderlies who had come to her rescue.

It was neither. Instead, the bed lay empty, shoved against the wall. Harper loomed over her attacker menacingly, his back to her. She couldn't see his face. What she *could* see was his ass as it played peek-a-boo through the back of the hospital gown.

On a normal day, the absurdity of the moment would have had her chuckling. Except this wasn't at all funny. The threat of violence lay like a mantle over the soldier's broad shoulders, just waiting to manifest. And...her brow creased. He appeared to be growling.

A shiver ran down her spine, dancing merrily on each vertebra as it went. Harper's hands clenched and unclenched at his sides as he stood over the doctor. As if he fought hard for control.

Lillian knew she should run. Raise the alarm. They had a patient loose. One who was, by the looks of it, capable of extreme violence. She could scream again, of course, but that wouldn't cut it. They were a mental hospital. Screams were as common as cheap linoleum and the scent of pine fresh antibacterial cleaner.

Walker shook his head, expression groggy. He lifted a hand to the back of his head. His eyes widened as it came away dark with blood.

"What the...?"

He looked up before going stock still as he registered

Harper stood over him. The blood drained from his face. She'd heard the phrase "as white as a sheet", but she'd never actually seen it. Until now.

"Fuck."

In a heartbeat, the doctor was all movement, scrambling up the wall as he tried to pull something from the pocket of his white coat. A gun. *Shit, he has a gun.* Lillian tried to call out a warning to Harper, but her vocal chords refused to cooperate. Her hand crept up to her throat. It was like a train wreck. She couldn't stop it or look away.

The soldier didn't need her warning. At the first sign of movement from Walker, he was already moving. His hand lashed out, open-palmed, in a slap instead of the punch she expected.

A small object flew out of Walker's grasp and clattered against the single cabinet in the room. The doctor howled in pain and hugged his hand to his body as he sagged against the wall again. A wet, red darkness spread over his lab coat as he glared defiantly at Harper. She covered her mouth with her hand, staring at the blood. How had Harper done that? He had to have a knife.

"Screw you," Walker spat in a voice thick with hatred as he cradled the injured hand. "You're fucked. Doesn't matter if you turn me or kill me. They know the place is infected now. They'll level it with you and the little bitch inside."

She walked over, leaned down and picked up the object. Small and square, it was an electronic device of some type. A small red light blinked ominously on the side, echoing the menace in Walker's words.

"Infected? Infected with what?" she croaked as her voice finally decided to cooperate. What was Walker going on about? This was a hospital—they were very careful about any possible infections.

The fallen doctor laughed. Blood bubbled on his lips. Bright red, frothy blood. Lilly frowned. She'd seen blood from many sorts of wounds, and this looked wrong. It looked fake. She knew it wasn't. Blood that color meant that too many things were wrong inside for the patient to survive.

"You really don't get it, do you, sweetheart?" Walker wheezed as his breathing became more labored. What was going on? He shouldn't have respitory problems from a hand wound. "Your precious captain here, and the rest? They're not nutcases...they're experiments. Military experiments. Lycanthropes. Where else do you think we could put them so no one would listen to a word they said, apart from a mental institute?"

Lillian laughed nervously as she stepped closer, all her instincts on high alert. Harper still had his back to her, so she couldn't see his face. The seriousness of her situation started to sink in. If Walker was lying, then she was in a cell with a lunatic who'd just wounded a doctor with a knife he'd smuggled in. If what said Walker was the truth, she was in a cell with God knew what... Military experiment? Even the phrase had a bad ring to it.

Crap. She knew she should've stayed in bed this morning.

Blood. It called to him in a seductive voice. Jack stood his ground against its lure. Despite what they'd done to him, he was not an animal. Not a dog to be swayed by the scent of fresh meat, or tempted by the delectable treat that stood behind him.

Blood lust and lust of the more carnal kind fought for dominance, their battlefield his taut frame. His mouth full of lengthened canines, he couldn't answer the doctor's accusations. Not until he could talk normally. But what was he going to say, anyway? *Sorry darlin', everything Psycho Doc here says is true*?

Yeah, like she would believe he wasn't a nutcase right there.

Walker looked at him with glee even as the drugs to counter lycanthrope infection destroyed his system from the inside out. The Project's top dogs were so scared of the virus being transmitted outside their test group that they pumped the rest of the staff full of some pretty serious shit to avoid them becoming infected. Unfortunately, it was a terminal solution. The drugs stopped them from becoming infected, true, but they also terminated any other sign of life.

"See? He's a fucking dog. Practically pissing himself because he can smell blood and a hot woman. He'll be wagging his tail and rolling over to let you rub his tummy next. Isn't that right, mutt?" Walker's voice turned scornful as he waved the hand Jack had shredded, splattering the floor in front of him with fat droplets of blood.

He couldn't help it. Jack fixated on those red drops. His mouth watered. All his instincts screamed at him to pounce and slash...tear skin and muscle until the blood ran thick and hot. Gulp it and chunks of flesh down until the endless hunger in his gut was assuaged.

"Captain Harper? Are you okay?"

Her voice behind him was the only thing that stopped the rising hunger, kept him from launching himself at Walker and tearing the man limb from limb to feast on his still twitching corpse. Jack traded one lust for another as his beast fixated on her instead. Female. Hot, sexy, fertile...he could read it all from her scent. An elusive, erotic fragrance that was hers and hers alone.

"Run, Little Red Riding Hood, run. Before the Big Bad Wolf

eats you all up!" Walker cackled, sliding farther down the wall. He was gray. Jack could smell death on him as surely as if the Grim Reaper were in the room with them.

"First he was a dog, now he's a wolf. Make your frigging mind up. And for heaven's sake, let's get some pressure on that wound. Where'd you get your license, off the back of a cereal box?" Lillian snapped as she grabbed a dressing from the nearby counter and stepped toward Walker.

Jack half-started toward her, reaching out to grasp her arm in an iron grip he tried to gentle. Touching *any* man, even a dying one, was a bad thing. The creature inside him wouldn't tolerate his woman touching another. Touching Walker, with his infected blood, would be more trouble than she'd dreamed of.

"No point—" Walker coughed up more blood. Black this time. It didn't stop when he finished coughing, dripping like oil from the corners of his lips. "Dead already."

As soon as the words left his lips, Walker gasped. His body froze before his back arched in a hideous curve. The sharp staccato sound of his vertebrae snapping one after the other filled the room. With a final rattling moan, he slumped to the floor. Silent. The pool of darkness under him spread wider before it stopped.

"I-is he…?"

Lillian's hand covered her throat, distress rolling off her in waves.

"Don't look. He's gone."

He tucked her head against his shoulder, wrapping her in his arms and murmuring soothing sounds against her hair. In the face of her distress, his tenuous control strengthened, as though the creature within was content just being near her. He paused, savoring the new sensation. So used to the thing raging in anger and resentment, feeling it calm and almost content was a novelty.

It wouldn't last long, he knew that. Walker had called in the cavalry, but these particular reinforcements wouldn't be riding to anyone's rescue. Certainly not his or Lillian's, that was for sure. Walker had triggered the alarm, alerting Project Headquarters of a possible Lycanthrope infection. They wouldn't mess around. There would be no quarantine, no medical tests to evaluate the hospital staff for possible infection. The Project had only one way to deal with an unsanctioned lycan infection…

Termination.

It would take them a while to triangulate the signal and link it to Walker. Then they'd spend time trying to raise the guards here. Guards Jack had to deal with, and fast. Adrenalin and the need for violence, never far away, rose again.

"Come on, sweetheart, there's nothing we can do for him."

Dropping a kiss on the top of Lillian's hair, he guided her from the room. She shook, a fine tremor running through her slender frame. He wanted to wrap her in his arms and tell her it would all be okay, but he'd be lying. It wasn't going to be okay. It was never going to be okay again. She'd seen too much, stepped into his world at the worst possible moment.

And, thanks to Walker, she could never leave.

Chapter Three

"Hiya, beautiful. What can I do for you today?"

The cheerful greeting never changed. Major Antonia Fielding, Toni to her friends if she had any left, let the door swing shut behind her and walked farther into the lion's den.

The medical center on-site was state of the art. Despite the appearance of the buildings outside, weather-beaten concrete that had definitely seen better days, the inside had been gutted and refitted when the Project had moved in.

Now gleaming steel workbenches filled the labs she'd passed. They contained all manner of equipment for the modern-day Frankensteins that moved between them shrouded in white protective suits. All contained behind the safety glass that kept unauthorized personnel, like her, out. Most of it she had no chance of identifying, even if she wanted to. And the medical bay itself could have doubled as a set for the Starship Enterprise.

Feeling like the little pig heading right into the wolf's lair, she walked up the middle of the room. Neatly made beds lined the walls, each one framed by its own set of curtains, like a masterpiece on display in the Louvre. Her gaze skittered away from the restraints. That sight, more than anything else, brought home that this wasn't your average medical center. It wouldn't be, couldn't be, because the camp itself was anything but normal.

The patients were definitely unusual.

She hated hospitals and medical bays. Hell, she even stayed away from first aid kits. She hated anything that had to do with the scientific or medical professions. Far from being the sources of comfort and help they were for the human population, they had caused her nothing but pain and misery. Oh, yes...

That would be because she wasn't human.

Not anymore.

"The usual," she answered, short and clipped, as she reached the last bed, the only one with a trolley next to it, and sat down. She didn't want to be here. In fact, she'd have happily crawled over broken glass if it meant she could get out of here quicker.

"Short, sweet and always to the point. That's what I like about you, Major."

Garry Stevens, her med tech, smiled and turned to the trolley at his side. It was covered with a green drape, but Antonia didn't need to see to know what was on it. Her enhanced sense of smell picked up the astringent scent of the antiseptic wipes in their packaging and the cloying sweetness of the already prepared shot. Underneath it, she could detect a lingering hint of the cleaner they'd used on the floor and, to the left, dead blood from the yellow syringe bin.

Bile rose in a hot wave as her body tried to expel the little she'd eaten that morning. "Yeah, I'm just that freaking likable."

She closed her eyes and swallowed. Everything inside her rejected the smell. It smelled wrong...it would hurt, make her ill. Grimly, she forced the wayward thoughts down and locked them away. The medication wouldn't make her sick—that was the disease talking. The medication made her better, took away the terrible cravings that gnawed at her gut and stole her self-control.

Holding onto that thought, she shifted until she lay on the bed.

Garry looked her over, his human-blue eyes assessing the tension in her slender frame. He'd been her tech as long as she'd been coming here, since the incident that made her the way she was, so he knew her of old.

"Do you need the restraints? Just to hold onto? After all this time, I don't think I need to fasten them. Do you?"

His voice soft and concerned, he reached into his pocket and pulled out a penlight. With swift, efficient movements he checked her pupil dilation. She winced and tried not to pull away from the light. It felt like the guy was stabbing a hot poker right through her pupils. *Bright light, bright light,* her instincts screamed, urging her to run for the nearest and deepest shadows. Her lips quirked at her own inner dialogue. Yeah, feed her after midnight and there would be trouble.

"You're a bit fixed, reactions are slow. Have you been feeding properly?"

Toni ignored the question as she felt across the bed. Her fingertips contacted the nylon webbing and padding of the restraints. She grabbed hold, testing their strength. They slid but held, just. The bed underneath, designed for patients like Toni, barely moved. There was just the tiniest squeak as one wheel rolled against its brake.

"Major…have you been feeding on schedule? You know how important that is," Garry chided as he took her wrist and started to time her pulse. "Your pulse rate is up as well."

She wrinkled her nose. She hated feeding. The stuff they gave them to eat was cold and unappetizing. Dead, and it smelled that way, turning her stomach no matter how hungry she was.

"I try."

He sighed as he pushed her sleeve up her arm and swabbed down her skin with a wipe. She didn't look as he picked up the needle. She hated this part. Her heart picked up its pace. If she weren't careful it might hit ten beats a minute.

She hissed as the needle punctured her skin and slid into the vein. Her entire arm throbbed as he depressed the plunger and the sickly-pink liquid inside pushed into her bloodstream.

His blue eyes watched her, sharp as a hawk. The look of concern he'd worn earlier had disappeared, replaced by focused interest. Toni lay back on the bed as the medication invaded her system. No matter how friendly and flirtatious Garry seemed, she had to remember he was a scientist through and through, and she wasn't human. She was a subject.

Classification: Blood-infected human.

Translation: Vampire.

"Hey, what the fuck do you think you're up to? You can't bring that through here. This is a live treatment area!"

Garry's voice, sharp with panic and anger, cut through the post-med fuzz in Antonia's head like a buzzsaw. They had her on the highest concentration now, and it took a toll on her system. For half an hour after her shots, she was out of it, playing with the fairies.

It was worth it if the damn stuff took the edge off the terrible hunger that ate at her day and night. The sort of hunger that had her looking at Garry's neck and seeing an all-you-can-drink buffet.

She fought her way back through the pink fuzz and ignored the purple elephants dancing at the edge of her vision. Some fucktard had thought it would be funny to play a Disney DVD during one of her shots, and now pink elephants plagued her as soon as the stuff was pushed into her veins. If he wasn't already dead, she'd rip his damn throat out. Sliding her tongue along an elongated canine, she smirked. She sure had the right dental equipment.

"I'm serious. You cannot bring that through here. Not with Bloods around..."

The stench reached Antonia, its fetid fingers reaching out and winding around her, pressing against her skin and leaving an oily residue. She sat bolt upright, a growl in the back of her throat as the smell bypassed any higher mental functioning and triggered her baser instincts.

Unfortunately, they weren't her human ones.

"It's okay, Major. Calm down."

Garry placed a gentle hand on her arm. She wasn't sitting on the bed anymore, but crouched on top of it, her legs bunched under her and her fangs bared as she prepared to leap. How had that happened?

She slid him a sideways glance, but her gaze was pulled back to the other side of the room like a magnet. A medical orderly stood in the doorway, his expression a mixture of defiance and fear as he stared at her. She didn't blame him. One of the oldest Bloods on camp, her abilities had been tested, recorded and proven in the field.

Her attention wasn't on him, though. He was just window dressing. It was all on the gurney he pushed in front of him, complete with black standard-issue body bag. Her lip curled back from her teeth again.

To the human eye it looked like a dead body in a bag. Hell, to her enhanced sight it looked like a body in a bag. But sight wasn't her primary sense. It had given way a long time ago to her sense of smell. And *that* was telling her the thing inside the bag wasn't dead. Not by a long shot. Soon it would rise again, but it wouldn't be alive.

"It's dead," the orderly argued. "The stuff didn't take. It's as dead as a doornail."

Garry shook his head, his hand still on her arm. "You *still* can't bring it through here. Nor any of the live areas."

"Awww, come on, man. I'm only going to the incinerator. It's cut through here or walk all the way around."

"Walk all the way around." Garry's voice was hard and uncompromising. "They've got Lycans in the next ward. You really want to walk through there?"

The orderly paled, all of the blood leeching from his face. For a vampire, it was a fascinating sight, like the stuff had decided to play hide-and-seek. She shook her head to clear it. When she started to think blood was being coy, she definitely needed more to eat.

"No, I thought not. Now get that down to the incineration chamber. Sometimes they take a while, so if I were you, I'd want to get that thing safely roasted before it can start walking about."

She watched as Garry shivered when the orderly yanked the gurney back through the door. The loose wheel squealed in protest and faded as he disappeared down the corridor at speed.

"I fucking *hate* those things."

Antonia arched an eyebrow. "Orderlies?"

He shot her a look, as though he couldn't work out if she was serious or joking. Finally, he chuckled and ran a hand through his hair. She realized with surprise that he was shaking. The little incident really did have him on edge.

"They're bad enough…but no. The re-animates."

Slowly she sat down again, interested despite herself. She shouldn't be. Shouldn't even be talking to him. There was a rule about no interspecies fraternization on camp. The kind of rule that didn't just get a smack on the wrist, it got people dead or locked up. In this place, locked up was as good as dead considering what people got locked up with.

Garry was nice, though. She liked him. Insomuch as it was possible to like someone who stabbed you on a regular basis.

"You work with Bloods. Vampires," she pointed out. "We're infinitely more dangerous than any of the RAs."

"Yeah, I know. But you guys are different." Flicking her a glance as if to check the likelihood she would freak out on him, he started to clean up his trolley. "With you, there's human intelligence, reasoning. As long as you're not in blood lust, we're all good. Even..." His voice lowered as he concentrated on cleaning down the bare steel with anti-bac. Avoiding her gaze.

"Well. It wouldn't be too bad if I *did* get infected in here. You're kinda cool," he admitted. "But to be like *that*. Just a mindless zombie. I can't even look at them. Patterson's a freak, he loves the zombies."

She slid off the treatment couch with an economy of movement she knew the human staff found disturbing and looked at him levelly.

"Garry, I'll give you one piece of advice because you're the nearest thing I have to a friend. Get out while you can. This place isn't career advancement. It's not even career death. It really *will* kill you."

Before Garry could answer, his cheeks a bright flaming banner of discomfort, the speaker overhead squawked into life.

"Major Fielding, please report to the Operations office. That's Major Fielding to the Operations office. Thank you."

No rest for the wicked. Inclining her head to Garry in an

Old World gesture she'd acquired rather than been born with, she turned toward the door. She couldn't wait to get out of the medical center, but she refused to run. She didn't run. Not now. After all, the worst had already happened, so what was left to run from?

The door opened just before she got to it, and two chattering women stepped through. Human, camp admin staff. As soon as they saw her, the chatter died on their lips. The one in front looked nervously at the red patch on Antonia's arm and paled.

"It's okay, Sylvie," her companion reassured, trying to peel the other woman off the wall. "It's just a Blood. It won't hurt you. Morning, Major, everything all right?"

"Perfectly, thank you. You two have a good morning," she answered politely. She scolded herself to behave, but she couldn't resist temptation. She smiled as she passed the two, baring her fangs. While not as impressive at rest as when they were fully extended, they were still enough to make the first woman whimper in fear.

Antonia grinned as she pushed through the door and into the open air. Her grin quickly died as she squinted in the bright sunlight. Whipping out a pair of shades, she shoved them onto her face and wished for rain.

She used to love the sun, always out basking in it. These days she'd be happy with a permanent raincloud directly overhead. Her own personal sunscreen. Unlike the films, the sun didn't turn her into crispy critter. She was still trying to work out if it was a blessing or a curse. It wasn't as if she got a cool sword a la *Blade* for being a daywalker. Instead she'd gained an unquenchable thirst, fangs that would make a *Twilight* fan green with envy and a red patch on her uniform sleeve so anyone looking could see what manner of creature she was.

On the plus side, at least she didn't sparkle. That would just add insult to injury.

Suppressing a shudder at the very thought, she turned right and headed for the Operations office. Not a long walk from the medical center, but long enough. Especially at this time of day, when all of the camp staff were out and about for lunch. Not that it made much difference to Antonia. She never had to wait in line or walk around people. As soon as those in front of her registered the red patch on her arm, her very own scarlet letter, they parted like the sea in front of Moses.

Her lips quirked bitterly at her train of thought. She'd been brought up to believe in God. As a child she'd attended Sunday school. She could recite the Lord's Prayer back to front and upside down. And where had He been when she needed him?

Nowhere to be fucking found, that's where.

She'd tried to talk to the camp Padre after her accident. The guy's eyes had about bugged out of his head when she'd walked in, and the conversation had gone downhill from there on out. It seemed that, as far as the Padre and his God were concerned, Antonia Fielding had died the day she'd become infected. According to them, the creature she had been transformed into was nothing more than an abomination, something to be destroyed rather than suffered to live.

The anger and hatred in his eyes had taken her aback. If she hadn't held onto her self-control, the Padre could have found himself in the same boat faith-wise...up shit creek without a paddle.

Shaking herself out of her memories, she carried on walking. Her long, loose-limbed stride ate up the path between her and the Operations office. Around her, the low buildings of the camp hugged the ground in defense against the harsh desert conditions. That was another thing she couldn't wrap her head around. The Project had housed Vampires, creatures known for their general intolerance to sunlight, out in the freaking desert. Talk about the last place people would expect to find them.

The skin between her shoulder blades prickled as she turned the next corner. Her destination lay up ahead on the left, but to her right stood a holding pen. She looked up, directly into a pair of amber eyes. Instinctively, her lip started to curl back as she recognized the man that stood behind the silver-laced steel for what he was.

Lycan. Wolf. Just as infected as her, but with a different strain of the virus. Not content with creating a new species of Nosferatu, the scientists had decided to play God again. The Lycanthropes were the result. A growl rose in the back of her throat, a sound of malevolence matched by the man in the cage. His eyes followed her as she walked up the path, resentment shining in their inhuman depths. Lycans were less stable than even the most whacked-out Blood, so they had to be caged. For their safety...no, that was bullshit. The Lycans were locked up for the safety of everyone else.

"Fucking Project lapdogs," she hissed and pushed open the doors of the Operations office to find out who she had to kill this time.

Chapter Four

She couldn't believe she was crying. Lillian didn't cry. Ever. She was tougher than that. Tougher than the stereotypical little woman who fell apart at the first sign of danger... Or the mother who couldn't cope after the death of her husband and hightailed it to her lover with teary demands to "make the nightmare go away". And conveniently forgot the fact she'd left her baby daughter behind.

She was not that woman, nor anything like her.

Once in the corridor, away from the stench of death and the sight of all that black, *wrong* blood, she stepped away from Jack and swiped at her tears with the back of her hand. Despite the fact he'd just killed a man, there was something about him that made her feel safe. Safe with a murderer. Okay, now she *knew* she was losing it. Perhaps insanity ran in her family and they'd just never told her?

"I'm sorry. I'm not normally like this," she apologized as she looked up and offered a small, teary smile. Her mouth already open to explain, she stopped.

He was gorgeous.

She'd known that. When they'd brought him in, her mind had told her that he was sex on a stick. But he'd been injured, a patient. Even though she was the hospital manager, she was bound by the patient-doctor thing, surely? The one that said "thou shalt not lust after the patients".

Now though, without all the blood and the ragged uniform—even in the hospital gown that did nothing for anyone—he was so good-looking it took her breath away. She shook her head slightly, waiting for the hidden cameras and some cheesy reality show host to burst out of the supply cabinet in the corridor next to them. He couldn't be for real. Soldiers just didn't look that good.

With warm amber eyes set above sharp cheekbones, his face was bisected by a strong, straight nose over sensually full lips. A severe buzz-cut merely highlighted his attractiveness, concentrating all attention on his face. He should be strutting his stuff on a catwalk, not getting down and dirty playing soldier.

Her eyes travelled downward, and the rest of him more than fulfilled the promise of his face. He was toned...hell no, he was *ripped.* Even his muscles had muscles. Tall and broad shouldered, he was built like a quarterback, and his life had obviously been one of violence. Old scars dotted his skin like a mad artist had gone to town with his body as the canvas.

"I know you're not. You're strong."

His words drew her attention back to his face. His eyes were blue again. He smiled, which almost robbed her of reason, but she held onto the thought for grim death. No one's eyes changed that fast. *What the hell have they done to him?*

"Your eyes... What the hell are you?"

The smile turned cold, his features freezing around it and locking it into place. In hindsight, perhaps a demand for information wasn't the best way to deal with this, especially after what had gone on in the room behind them. Walker was slumped, dead, but somehow she knew Jack wouldn't hurt her.

He moved toward her. Only three steps, but with those blue

eyes intent upon her, it seemed more like a stalk. With every movement he made, her instincts screamed "predator".

She held her ground, tilting her head to look at him as he neared. He stopped inches away from her, so close the heat of his body beat at her skin even through her clothing and his gown.

"We don't have time for this, Lilly."

He lifted a hand to tuck a loose strand of hair behind her ear. As though he couldn't stop touching her, he stroked a gentle finger down her cheekbone to the corner of her lips. It took everything she had not to turn her head and press into the small caress, but she held true to her purpose, her eyes on his.

"Make time."

His lips quirked, and everything female in her went into meltdown. He had to know the effect he had on women, so she ignored the reaction and met him look for look.

"Stubborn little minx."

She choked. "What did you call me?"

"Minx," he repeated, lowering his head and brushing his lips over hers to silence her. As a tactic, it worked. The first touch of his lips, warm and firm over hers, was like setting light to kindling. Heat flared and caught, racing through her body like wildfire.

She moaned, unable to stop her lips parting automatically in invitation. No matter what her mind was screaming about the dead guy in the next room and the possibility the hunk stood in front of her wasn't just human, her body knew what it wanted, and what it intended to get.

He didn't pass up the invitation. Groaning, he moved closer and deepened the kiss. With a ruthless sweep of his tongue, he parted her lips farther and slid into the softer recesses of her mouth. She shivered, hot and cold chills chasing over her skin as he kissed her in the darkness of the corridor.

She'd been kissed before and, as she'd thought anyway, she'd been kissed well. This was something else entirely. He kissed her as if there was nothing else in the world. As if she was his sun, his moon and stars...his everything. He didn't kiss her, he made love to her with his lips and tongue.

Abruptly he broke away, tearing his mouth from hers. With a groan of frustration, he leaned forward to rest his forehead against hers.

"I don't want to let you go." The tone in his voice pulled on her heartstrings. "When they brought me in, there was just pain and blood...so much blood. Darkness was coming for me, and I was ready. But an angel called my name... I had to come back to see if she was as beautiful as she sounded."

His words reached deep inside her. She already thought he was gorgeous, but to have him spouting words that...romantic wasn't the word. The claim he'd come back just to see her, that hit her deep down and resonated in her soul.

"And...?"

She almost dared not ask the question, and when she did, her voice emerged breathy and hopeful. Like a teen finally meeting and speaking to her film idol in the flesh.

"Oh yes, she was worth it."

"Hey you, what are you—holy shit! Sound the alarm, the Alpha's loose."

Fuck...ing hell. Just what he needed.

Jack sighed and stole another kiss. Just one. Nothing more than a peck on her lusciously soft lips. He couldn't linger, couldn't risk it. He needed to deal with those guards now. Even after he'd had his guts shredded and pushed a truckload of silver out through his pores, two guards were little more than a light workout. The rest he'd rather pick off one by one, preferably before the call came in from Project headquarters to check in on Walker's pager alert.

Putting temptation aside, he tucked Lillian behind the steel supply cabinet. What she'd seen with Walker was just the tip of the iceberg. She didn't need to see this, didn't need to see the full horror of his animal side. Not yet.

"Stay put. Don't look," he ordered in an undertone. "Hey guys." He held his hands out to the side as he started walking toward the two guards at the end of the corridor. Both looked like rabbits caught in the headlights. "How's it hanging?"

Adrenalin pumped through his body as he walked, feet cold on the linoleum flooring. Within him, his beast howled and yammered to be free. To burst from the confining human form and race down the corridor free.

Even dulled by this shape, his expanded senses fed him information. He could smell their fear. Hear the pounding of their hearts in twin panicked rhythms. Sense the hot rush of blood just under their skin.

"Stay right there."

One of them managed to snap out of it, fumbling with the pistol holstered at his hip. When he managed to pull the weapon free, his hand shook.

"I—I'm not kidding. Drop and spread 'em. Or—or else!"

Jack kept walking. His body surged with power, the stresses of the last forty-eight hours gone as if they'd never been. The moon was up, his mate was within reach and he felt good. A low snarl rumbled up from his chest. Forget lean, mean fighting machine. He was lethality in motion.

Not stopping, he reached inside himself and opened the

cage that kept the beast confined. Just a little, no more than a crack. Power and pain flooded through him in equal amounts, filling his body and surging through his veins like molten metal.

"Or else what?"

His voice was low, gruff. More like a growl than human. Both guards had been with the Project long enough to know what that meant.The acrid stink of fresh urine filled the corridor as the one on the left pissed his pants.

His teeth clenched, he grabbed the fiery wolf by its tail and molded it, shaping it to his needs and his will. *Change, change, change.* He forced the shift down to his hands. Bones cracked, breaking as they lengthened. Skin slid and popped over the changing shape. His fingers stretched, talons sprouting until he sported a set that would make any self-respecting wolfman pale in envy.

He didn't give them a chance to reply. The next step brought him within striking distance. The guard on the right gasped, the muzzle of his gun shaking as he started to squeeze the trigger. The one on the left fumbled with the restraining clip on his holster.

Jack's eyes narrowed, his world focused on that finger and its progress as it tightened. Time slowed to a crawl, the corridor around them went gray and out of focus. He moved, his motions seeming slow as the seconds spun out. He swept his arm up in an arc, claws fully extended.

The pistol clicked as the trigger reached first pressure. The tiny sound was like a gunshot to his sensitive ears. His human brain fed him what was happening inside the pistol, but his animal side didn't care. Talons connected, cutting through skin, muscle, sinew, and bone like a hot knife through butter as he completed the arc.

The pistol fired. Screams filled the corridor. The smell of

blood blossomed, full and heavy. Cordite joined it, the two blending into an evocative smell that teased his wolf into a blood-frenzy.

Jack didn't let it. He held onto control by the thinnest of threads, aware of the woman hiding behind the heavy metal cabinet. With bullets flying around as they were, the last thing he needed was her loose and in the mix. It would only take a stray bullet...

Using the power he'd unleashed, he channeled it into action. The guard's hand bounced off the floor, leaving a red smear as it rolled. Jack ignored it, side-stepping to land a solid kick in the injured guy's gut. He went down, curling around his damaged arm like a fetus in the womb. Already he was starting to fit, his body stiffening as the drugs in his system reacted to the Lycan infection introduced by Jack's claws.

Jack didn't stop moving. Using his momentum, he bounced off the floor and back up into the attack. The second guard didn't clear leather before Jack was on him. He grabbed the hand covering the weapon and wrenched it loose, holster and all. It slammed into the wall behind them with a dull thud at the same time Jack twisted the guard's wrist out from his body.

With a quick spin, he had the smaller man in the cradle of his embrace. But even if Jack had been so inclined, this was no lover's clinch. His free hand smoothed over the guys throat, the razor sharp claws tickling over his Adam's apple as it bobbed up and down. He babbled unintelligibly, another wave of urine stench washing over him as he lost control of his bladder again. Jack felt no pity. This was the guy who'd laughed in the blood wagon when Jack's guts were on display.

"Too slow. Way too slow. You should have picked another career," he whispered and drew his claws lightly across the man's throat. The cut wasn't serious—it barely broke the surface. A solitary bead of blood rolled down to the starched uniform collar.

The wound wouldn't kill him, but it was still a death sentence.

Even though, she had to be up and around during the day, Antonia was very much a nocturnal creature. She could tolerate the sun, and indeed had to, but for the most part it left her wanting to curl up and sleep somewhere warm.

Garry had told her it was because her body had changed. He'd thrown big words around, but the basics had boiled down to the fact she'd switched to cold-blooded rather than warm. Her metabolism, always high, had gone into meltdown. When active, her readings were off the chart, but if she wanted to she could just stop, shutting everything down until she resembled an incredibly detailed, lifelike statue.

To say it freaked out the medical staff was an understatement, and Antonia was probably the only person ever to have been barred from the camp mess hall.

Ops had only wanted her to sign off on reports. Paperwork never quit, even when you were "dead" to all intents and purposes. Still fully clothed, she lay on the bed and stared at the ceiling. The room was small but private. At first she'd thought it a luxury; now she realized it was little more than another prison. Sure, the lock on the door had been deactivated now, but it hadn't always been. In the early days, just after her "accident", they'd locked her in here from sundown to sunup on the thinking that she and the rest of the Bloods were less dangerous during the day.

A snort of amusement escaped her. Yeah right, the day any Blood was harmless was the day Barney became President.

She went back to counting paint blots above her. She'd been up all day, but sleep was proving to be elusive. Counting paint blots was marginally better than counting sheep. Counting sheep became counting bags of blood running around on little woolly legs. Which made her hungry, made her fangs drop and burn, and soured her temper even more than normal.

She tilted her head...had that been two or three blots? She counted it as two and moved on. Interestingly, since her accident, she hadn't had PMS or even a period. One of the upsides of being a vampire, because even *she* wouldn't want to see a vamp with PMS.

The room lights were off, but she didn't need light to see. Another benefit of her new existence. At least it would be if normal light didn't give her a blinding headache. The sort of headache that felt like a spitfire was trying to take off inside her head, and no amount of over the counter medicine could deal with it.

At three hundred blots, a door opened down the hall and footsteps sounded in the corridor outside. Stopping her count, she listened as they approached. Lifting her chin, she scented the air. Human, male and scared out of his wits. The scent of fear clogged the air, like thick incense.

Three doors away. Two doors.

How had they gotten a human to come down here at this time of night? It was bad enough trying to get them to come in here in the daylight, when they were all safe and secure in the knowledge that vampires were "docile" in the day. Yeah right... She gargled holy water and shit garlic.

One door, and the footsteps carried on. Antonia held her breath and waited for the sharp rap on her door.

"Major Fielding? You're needed in the Operations office."

Without conscious thought, she was off the bed and headed

for the door. The guy the other side, a corporal, yelped and jumped as she yanked it open less than a second after he'd spoken.

"For? I do sleep, you know."

She glared at him, the look in her eyes deliberately glacial. Even though she hadn't been asleep and his arrival was a welcome distraction from her contemplation of the ceiling's paint job, she was still offshift. A familiar resentment filled her. She was fed up with the Project snapping its fingers and expecting her to jump.

"Uhmm…they didn't say. J-just that you're needed." The corporal paled, appearing to realize that he stood in the middle of vampire country, facing down the queen bitch herself. The pissed-off queen bitch.

A bead of sweat ran from his hairline and rolled down his brow. His gaze shifted sideways to the door.

"You'd never make it in time," she informed him softly, amused that any human thought he could outrun her. He paled even further, his lip quivering. Antonia shook her head and decided to give him a break. He was so scared that baiting him seemed cruel. *Like kicking a puppy.*

"Operations? We may as well go."

Stepping out through it, she pulled the door shut behind her and started to walk up the corridor. It was a long walk to the outer door, the expanse of wall broken at regular intervals by doors. Each had a lock. Most were active.

A low moaning sob emanated from the last one as they passed it. A sound of misery and hopelessness that evolved into rage and frustration, then back again. Antonia's jaw tightened. She recognized the sound of a newly turned Blood suffering their first thirst. Remembered the endless night she woke feeling like her body, her very blood, was boiling. The pain was excruciating, something she wouldn't wish on her worse enemy.

She'd drunk gallons of water, only to throw it back up. Soda tasted worse—fizzy acid. White wine? Paint stripper. There were only two things even slightly palatable: port and, of course, blood.

Chapter Five

It didn't take long to reach Operations. In point of fact, it didn't take long to walk across the entire camp. The part that was habitable, anyway. Built way back when, it had been abandoned for years before the Project had come along. Most of the buildings were still uninhabitable, apart from a main core around the central hub.

Well, inhabitable was a relative term, she thought as she passed the Lycan kennels. They'd thrown up some silver-banded steel fencing and let the dogs loose in what amounted to little more than huge dog pens. Her lip curled again as she passed, the stench wafting toward her on the night breeze. She wouldn't be surprised if they had to send someone in every day to muck them out.

"Freaking animals," she muttered, unable to keep her prejudice to herself. Before she'd become changed, she hadn't had any feelings one way or the other about Bloods or Lycans, other than the fact both freaked her out. They were all the same to her. People who'd been willing test subjects or those unfortunate enough to be infected. She hadn't counted on the fact that when the Project ran out of willing test subjects, it created its own.

And she certainly hadn't counted on the rush of complete and utter hatred the first time she'd seen a Lycan after her infection. Anger had welled up from her very core, as though her soul itself rejected the idea of the creature in front of her. Her fangs had dropped, despite the sedative they had her on, and it had taken all her self-control not to rip its throat out right there.

"Sorry?" The corporal leaned forward trying to catch her whispered words, a look of puzzlement on his face.

She shook her head and waved her hand in a dismissive gesture. "It doesn't matter."

Still, she shot a glance over her shoulder at the dark and silent Lycan pens as she walked through the door into the office. As far as she was concerned, every one of them should be put down. Taken out to the edges of the camp where they buried all the failed test subjects and shot point-blank in the back of the head with a silver bullet.

Hell, she'd offer to do it herself.

"Ah, Major. So good of you to join us."

Colonel Nathan Fitzgerald looked up with a smirk as Antonia entered the control room. Amusement glinted in his deep-set eyes, as though he knew she'd been pulled from her bed, and the power he had over her filled him with petty glee.

Deliberately, she blanked her expression and gave him a poker face to look at. She didn't like Fitzgerald, and she was sure the feeling was mutual. He was the sort of inbred, jumped-up son of a senator who never had to fight for anything in his life. A person for whom life opened doors by dint of association, who his parents were, rather than for anything he'd done or achieved himself. For a kid from the rough side of town who'd dragged herself up and fought for every chance she'd gotten, it was sickening. *He* made her sick.

He was also a bully. Rather than using his rank and position in the Project for good, for the technological and scientific advance that could be the *only* reason the government would do what they did to their own people, he used it to reinforce a whole new set of prejudices and racism based on his own opinion.

"As always, I live to serve."

Her voice, calm and collected, revealed nothing of her bitterness as she quoted the Project's motto back at him. *Live to serve.* In other words, *Your ass is ours. If we can bring you back as something else, we will, and you'd better be fucking grateful.*

He wasn't intelligent enough to read between the lines and figure out the sarcasm. Yet another worrying lack in a full-bird colonel.

"Good. Just make sure you remember that."

He pushed away from the planning table and looked her straight in the eye. Everything in Antonia went still. She recognized that look. The "you've fucked up" look.

"Of course, sir."

He had a pen in his hand, fiddling with it. *Click-click.* His thumb hit the end in a rapid-fire motion. *Click-click.* The pen nib appeared and disappeared. *Click-click.* The sound reverberated through her skull like the double-tap from a rifle. The tension in the room rose several notches as the other staff with them faded out of view. No one wanted to get between the colonel and his victim.

Antonia stood her ground and gave him a rattlesnake look. Her best. It made people...human people, that is...uncomfortable as hell. Something in their brains clicked on when she looked at them like that, and ramped their survival instincts up to maximum. Full-Bird Fiztgerald was just too fucking dumb to realize the danger signs when he poked at the tiger with a stick.

"I have always run this camp with fairness and equality in

mind, no matter what ethnic or species origin our staff are..."

Great, she was getting the equality and diversity speech. Someone, please shoot her now.

"But we do have to have some rules. Do you know what the most important of those rules are, Major?"

Time to play dumb grunt. She fixed her gaze to the wall behind Fitzgerald's shouldered and answered with an ambiguous, "Sir!"

It was a rhetorical question. He smiled, a particularly oily and smug expression she wanted to wipe off his face, preferably by knocking his teeth down his throat. Which she'd enjoy also ripping out.

"Our most important rule, given the different *species* on site, is to preserve the integrity of the human gene pool."

His irritating voice matched his smile. Patronizing and smug as he used big words as if she wouldn't know what he was talking about. Even if she didn't, she wouldn't give him the satisfaction of asking what he meant.

Her fixed look didn't waver. "Yes, sir. Of course, sir."

"You've not been a good girl and obeyed the rules, though. Have you, Major?"

That shocked her out of her rigid contemplation of the plaster behind him.

"Sir? I'm not sure what you mean."

A frown furrowed her brow as she looked him directly in the eye. A mistake. Those dark orbs set in heavy flesh that would turn into unhealthy-looking jowls within a few years glittered with a level of malevolence that took her aback. Malevolence aimed solely at her, yet not personal at all. Not only was she a woman in uniform, which was bad enough according to the camp's grapevine, but she was no longer human. And he hated anything not human.

"Oh, I think you know exactly what I mean."

The pen clicked again, four times. She wanted to ram it down his throat. Sideways.

"You've been fraternizing with some of the camp staff. The *human* staff. We have witnesses."

She couldn't help it. At his words, she barked out a laugh, a short, sharp sound of bitter amusement and surprise. She didn't *fraternize.* Hell, most of the time she didn't even smile. She'd rather tear most people's throats out than initiate conversation.

"Witnesses? To what?" She demanded, forgetting momentarily that he disliked being challenged. "Who are they?"

Fitzgerald waved his hand dismissively. "That doesn't matter. This infraction will go on your permanent record. If any more occur, action will have to be taken."

The screams died into whimpers of pain, which became chokes. Lillian stood where she'd been ordered behind the cabinet, flattened back against the wall. At first she'd been about to argue at his high-handed order, but then the gun had gone off.

All she could see was the furrow in the opposite wall. The bullet had taken the plaster out before burying itself in the wall at the end of the corridor. She'd helped deal with suicidal and violent patients, ones who struggled with the world in general and their place in it.

Being shot at was completely out of her realm of experience.

Men who weren't men, who sprouted claws the size of

bread knives that could shear a man's hand off at the wrist, were completely out of her realm of experience as well.

Right now she'd like her realm of experience to include being at home, tucked up in bed with a nice, safe chick flick in the DVD player. Which told exactly how out of her element she felt since she hated chick flicks with a passion. She favored action movies or the occasional horror. Watching horror, however, and taking a starring role were two completely different things.

She paled as the choking was interrupted by hideous cracking sounds. One after another, like rhythmic gunshots. She flinced with each crack. Without looking, she knew what was happening. In her mind's eye she could see the guards stiffening as their spines curved into the terrible arch Walker's had made. Arching until mere human anatomy gave under the strain and their vertebrae cracked, one after the other.

In fact, screw the chick flick. Right now she'd just settle for not being here in a corridor where men were dying. With the distinct likelihood she would join them in the very near future.

Oh my God. She had to get out of here. No matter how pretty Harper's words were, how much she felt they'd connected, he was a dangerous man...wolf...something. No matter how disenfranchised with the establishment a person was, there were ways and means of expressing your displeasure.

Killing people wasn't one of them.

The bone-crunching sounds stopped. Holding her breath, Lillian edged away from the wall and peeked around the cabinet. Jack stood a little way down the corridor, looking down at the two bodies. Like before, both lay in the middle of an ever-widening pool of black, brackish blood. She could smell the stuff from here. A chemical, *wrong* smell.

He stood between her and the entrance to the ward. Beyond the door behind him lay safety and more men with guns. Big guns. But first she had to get past him.

Still clad in the hospital gown, butt peeking through the gap, the mint green fabric was splattered in blood. His hands at his sides had reverted to normal, not the hideous claws she'd seen when she'd risked a glance around the corner. Just in time to see him do a slice and dice job on the first guard's hand.

A hand that lay a few feet away, the gun still in its grip. Funny that even when separated from the body, the hand had retained its last conscious position, finger curled around the trigger.

She needed that gun. Whether or not it would do any good against whatever Jack was, she didn't know. But being armed gave her a better chance of getting to the end of the corridor and out that door.

The fact that she'd never shot a gun in her life didn't cross her mind.

He still looked at the bodies, his head down between the broad width of his shoulders. They heaved, as though he were struggling for breath. Concern wrung her heart as she looked at the gun and back at him. Was he hurt? Had the guard shot him?

No, she'd definitely only heard one shot. There hadn't been time for a second before...she swallowed, the sound painfully dry...before he'd sliced the man's hand off.

Go, go, go, go... Her heart pounding, she forced herself into action. Legs bunched under her, she propelled herself out from behind the cabinet and toward her target. Shoulder slamming into the wall, she half slid down it as she grabbed up the gun and the severed hand. A small part of her brain yammered away as she tore the still-warm fingers loose and dropped the hand.

Clinical waste, she told herself. Not even an amputated limb since the body it belonged to was rapidly cooling, sans heartbeat, on the floor.

Her hand closed around the cool metal of the grip, her finger on the trigger, as if she'd used a gun every day of her life.

"Stay right where you are," she ordered, and tried to ignore her hand shaking.

He turned his head, his outline a silhouette against the light from the far door. His nostrils flared, but he didn't leap into action as she expected. She'd seen the speed he moved at. Way too fast to be human.

Arms out at his sides, which pulled the hospital gown in all sorts of interesting directions, he turned slowly to face her. She tightened her grip on the gun, trying to stop the tremble in her hand. Holding it tighter didn't work; the muzzle wobbled like Jell-O at a kid's birthday party.

"I mean it, freeze! On the floor, now!"

Her words had no effect. Instead of lying down as she'd ordered, he started to walk toward her instead. Fear raced through her body like a herd of wild horses.

"Shoot me if you need to, Lillian."

His voice was soft and gentle, filled with a tone that wrung her heart. As though he could meet hordes of armed guards with his bare hands and win, but that he couldn't, wouldn't, stop her.

"I don't blame you if you did. You've seen some of what I am, what I can do..." The gap between them shortened, his pace slow but inextricable. She took a pace back.

"And it gets worse. I'm the monster they made me, the creature of death and destruction they wanted. I've killed far more than these two. I'd like to say it was under orders...under the influence of the drugs they pumped into me...but it wasn't. I didn't know when I signed up what they were going to do. How it would change me."

Another step toward her, then another and another. Suppressing a whimper of fear, Lillian backed up, but he walked, talking all the time. *Shoot him,* her instincts screamed, but she couldn't. The pain in his rough voice wound around her heart, held her in thrall until her back hit the cold wall behind her.

"But I liked the killing. I liked letting this..." he thumped his chest, "...*thing* out. I had nothing to live for." He reached her, walking right up until the muzzle of the gun rested against his chest. Right over his heart.

"Until I saw you. You're perfect, sweetheart, everything I want...an angel I don't deserve. They..." He threw a snarl over his shoulder at the fallen men. "They knew what was coming if I got out. But if you choose to pull the trigger, I won't stop you. The bullet won't kill me—you'll need to shoot me in the head as well."

He smiled at her, sadness and something else...acceptance and another emotion she couldn't, didn't want to name, shining in his eyes. "Do it, sweetheart, let me have peace."

His words, the look in his eyes, reached right into her body and didn't just tear her heart out, they threw it on the floor and stomped on it for good measure. There was so much pain and resignation in his changeable eyes, seeing it brought tears to hers.

Just looking into his face, looking into his eyes, she felt as if she could see his soul. The soul of a man, not an animal. The animal the military scientists had put into him. That soul called to her, as though something in his gaze reached deep within her and flicked a switch. Trust flowed through her as she lowered the pistol.

Whatever he was, everyone deserved a second chance. But she'd keep hold of the pistol, just in case.

Jack held his breath as Lilly pressed the loaded pistol into the flesh of his chest. She was scared. Her beautiful eyes were wide, and her heart pounded so loudly he was surprised it didn't deafen her.

Her lip trembled, and she caught it between her teeth. The sight of that plump, pink flesh caught between her blunt, white teeth sent a bolt of lust through him so strong it almost brought Jack to his knees.

Fighting the urge back, he looked deep into her eyes. He saw the instant she made the decision that she couldn't pull the trigger. Relief, sharp and immediate, flooded his system as he reached out and gently removed the pistol from her shaking hand.

"Hey, it's okay, babe." He caught her easily as she sagged against him. Shivers racked her slender frame. He smoothed a big hand down the soft fall of her hair. Tiny and delicate, she fit perfectly against him, as though her body had been made to complement his.

His perfect mate.

"Sweetheart, I know this is a lot to take in, but we have to get moving." He hooked a finger under her chin to bring her eyes up to his. They were dilated. Shock. He recognized the signs. In truth, it amazed him she was holding up so well. Most women would have been a nervous wreck by now, but not his Lillian.

Gritting his teeth at the typical male reaction of his body, he eased away from her. She was already in shock, and they weren't out of the woods yet. The last thing she needed was to be confronted with the crass needs of his body. The animal inside him would push her up against the wall and take her here and now, with bodies and blood on the floor around them. The man in him refused to do that.

"Walker sent an alarm, they'll be sending in a clean-up team. We have to get everyone out of here before they arrive."

Chapter Six

Action will have to be taken.

Code words for the fact they'd drag her out to the edge of the camp and put a bullet through her brain. She might heal faster than a human, but no one could operate without most of their brain. Except a reanimate, of course.

With the trouble the Project went to in keeping the three areas of study separate, there was no way they'd use a blood-infected subject in one of the other trials. Besides, hard as they tried, neither Lycans nor Bloods could be turned re-animate. It was as though the infections already in their system overwhelmed the RA17 virus. Basically, once they were dead, they stayed dead.

"Yes, sir!"

She returned her gaze back to the same spot on the plaster and waited for the lecture to end, however long it took. The time made no difference to her. Without needing to sleep, eat or drink, she could keep this up for hours. Fitzgerald, however, would need to break at some point, if only to piss.

The colonel sighed, as though he'd guessed from her blank face he wasn't getting anywhere. *Hallelujah, he might actually possess some brains after all.*

"Okay, moving on. We have a situation that needs resolving. Sergeant…if you would, please."

One of the silent men in the room moved forward and spread a map over the table. As paranoid as a conspiracy theorist, the Project didn't trust computer networks and Internet link-ups. No, given the sensitive nature of the project they'd gone old-fashioned. Paper files couldn't be hacked into and spread over the Internet at the touch of a button.

Antonia snorted inwardly. Made sense—there was no way the government wanted the civilian population to know about experimentation on its own people.

"Okay, this is St. Mary's..." Fitzgerald announced as he stabbed his finger at an area on the map.

She leaned over the table slightly to get a look at the area he pointed to. A small estate set near what looked like a town. One road in and out, with forest and mountains to the east. Automatically, her tactical training kicked in. As a target, it was a good one to attack. She could already see the terrain in terms of troop movements and battle areas.

"It's the nuthouse we send the dogs to if they freak out. A furry funny farm." He laughed at his own joke. Antonia wondered how far she could bury his pen in his brain if she shoved it through one of his baby-blues.

"After all, no one gives a shit in there. Half the patients are convinced they're the President, and the other half Santa Claus. Compared to that, any stories of werewolves will just get them labeled nutjobs."

She nodded but didn't offer an opinion. As tactics went, it was sound. Use the system. It worked, until the lunatics ran the asylum.

"Something went wrong, though."

It wasn't a question, but a statement. She made sure to keep her tone level, neutral, so no inference about her personal feelings on the matter could be made. She didn't look at

Fitzgerald. Instead, she reached out and turned the map around to study it closer.

"Yeah...we think so," the sergeant spoke up, placing a clipboard on the table next to her. She pulled it toward her. It was an activity record. All project facilities kept in constant contact with headquarters. Hourly calls were made and received so that if the shit hit the fan, HQ knew within sixty minutes.

"No contact for an hour and a half? What's this here?" She pointed to a slip of paper clipped on the top.

"It's a remote alarm. Belonging to Dr. Walker. As soon as it was triggered we tried to initiate contact, but we haven't been able to raise anyone at the hospital."

She nodded. All her personal feelings about Fitzgerald and anyone else in the room melted away as duty took over. Antonia Fielding was first and foremost a soldier.

"Just Lycans on site?"

"From us, yes."

The silence after the sergeant's sentence was telling. Antonia looked up, her expression sharp and her eyes like a hawk's. The man shifted uncomfortably.

"Who else?"

"It's a general mental health facility as well. There's a civilian wing as well as an open wing."

She blinked once, slowly, and tried to figure out whether she'd really heard what she'd just heard. Or whether the Project really was stupid enough to send unstable Lycans into a facility with an open doors policy.

"An open wing? As in the patients can come and go at any time? And there are LY16 infected personnel there?" she asked, giving the Lycans their proper name and trying to avoid any hint of *What? Are you fucking crazy?* in her tone.

The sergeant gave her a blank face, but, unlike everyone else in the room, Antonia wasn't limited to the human senses. The sergeant's discomfort with the situation seeped out through his pores. He'd had curry last night. The pungent sweet-spicy aroma filled the room.

"The LY's are sectioned off into a secure wing. This is an old style asylum, right back from the Bedlam-type days of treatment."

Despite herself, she shuddered. Just the word conjured up images of patients strapped to beds, screaming in pain as they were subjected to electric shock treatment. They'd tried that on camp, very early on, under the premise that the electrical current could subdue the intense desires the Bloods, in particular, suffered.

Antonia had ripped the pads loose and threatened to shove them, and the machine, where the sun didn't shine. She hadn't been asked to "participate" in any further electric shock trials. In fact, she hadn't been asked to participate in trials at all since. Go figure.

"Okay, so we're assuming that no civilians are at risk?" She swung her monochrome-gaze around to encompass both Fitzgerald and the sergeant with all the answers.

Fitzgerald shook his head, his finger busily click-clicking on the pen. "You know what they say about assume..."

Antonia's expression deadened. If the next words out of his mouth were "it makes an ass out of you and me" she was not only going to ram that fucking pen up his ass but the entire map as well. Without lube.

Fitzgerald dropped his gaze and cleared his throat. "We can't assume anything. Not at this stage. All we know is we can't establish contact with an LY16 holding facility. I have authorization for a clean-up operation. We're about to start activating the RAs. Major, you'll be leading the operation."

She nodded. Since they'd dragged her out of bed at WTF o'clock, she'd assumed she'd be leading the operation. It wasn't her first clean-up, and she doubted it would be her last.

"The RAs aren't active yet? I'm assuming we're headed out by road?" She tapped the map idly. The hospital wasn't too far from the camp. A couple of hours hard drive and they'd be there.

Fitzgerald nodded and slipped his pen into his pocket. "Yes, air suppression teams are already in the air. Orders to shoot anything on foot and maintain a cordon around the hospital. Follow me. We'll head to the activation area. I think you'll want to see this."

"Of course, sir."

She hid her surprise and followed him without argument. This was new. Even as team commander she'd never been invited through to the activation area before, and as a Blood it was normally off limits to her, as were the Lycan labs. A feeling of unease filled her as she filed after them like a good little soldier. Whatever this was, it couldn't be good.

The sense of something wrong increased on the short walk through the maze that made the Operations building and had built into a fine crescendo as they entered the RA labs. By the time Fitzgerald opened the door to an observation room and gestured at her to precede him inside, not only had the hackles on the back of her neck risen, but the skin underneath was actively trying to crawl away as well.

What am I missing? What game is Fitzgerald playing now?

The room appeared empty, tables and chairs pushed against the wall behind the door. As always, she gave it a cursory glance before she stepped over the threshold. The look was a holdover from being human—these days, her enhanced senses told her the room was empty.

Like a moth drawn to the flame, she approached the window down the opposite side of the room. One-way glass, it didn't show the normal view of acrid desert outside. Instead she saw a darkened room below. For the people crowding in behind her, all of them human, it would have been impenetrable darkness. Not for a nocturnal creature. Her eyes had adapted to take advantage of the small amount of available light. Pupils dilating, the room below came into view. It was painted in shades of gray and black thanks to the darkness, but she easily made out the containment couches and the figures lying upon them.

Details emerged from the monochromatic view. She could make out the darker gray of the body bags each figure lay upon. Her logical mind filled in the orange they used for the RA body bags. Orange for RA, white for Lycan, black for Blood. Even after death, the Project worked at keeping the three strains separate.

Terrified moans reached through the thick plate glass. The lights snapped on, making her wince and squint. She cast a glance over her shoulder. Fitzgerald smirked as his hand left a bank of light switches. Her eyes narrowed as she contemplated killing him, slowly. She'd rip his throat out if she weren't convinced that stupidity, like the three viruses, was transmittable through blood.

"Oh my God, no. Please no. P-please…I beg of you. Don't do this."

The terrified whimper from the room stopped Antonia dead. Filled with utter terror, it was familiar. A man's voice.

Garry's voice.

It took her an eternity to turn, as she prayed that she'd heard incorrectly. It wasn't Garry. It couldn't be her med-tech, the guy who had looked after her since her accident, strapped to a bed with the rest and about to be turned into the living dead.

"Please...someone help me. There's been a mistake. I'm Garry Stephens. I *work* here!"

Her hope cut off dead as he said his name. He was in the middle, in full view from the window, flanked on each side by other couches. They were all occupied. Each had an orange jump-suited figure lying on an orange body bag. Color coordination, she liked it.

The other subjects lay silently, barely moving, with their eyes wide and pupils dilated. Death-row prisoners. All drugged out of their skulls to mimic the humane death they should have undergone. Instead, the Project had appropriated their bodies for "scientific research".

She snorted to herself. The government had always concealed weapons research under that banner. Garry was different, though. He wasn't drugged, still in the clothes she'd seen him in the day before, and terrified.

Her gaze snapped to Fitzgerald as he came to stand next to her. "What's he doing in there? He's a member of staff."

"I'm aware of that." The colonel turned his head to look at her, and Antonia read the answer in his eyes. Garry wasn't in there because he'd done anything wrong. He was there because of her.

He'd die for her mistake, whatever the hell it had been.

"Oh, for fucks sake. You can't do this."

Her words exploded out of her, escaping before she could censor them.

"If I've done something wrong, punish *me*. Not him."

"I think you need to remember who you're talking to, *Major*

Fielding."

Fitzgerald's voice seemed to whip out in the sudden silence of the room. Even Garry, on the other side of the thick plate glass, fell silent as though he could sense the standoff taking place mere feet from him.

"Dr. Stephens violated one of our prime directives within the Project and allowed himself to get too close to his subjects." Fitzgerald's lip curled as he raked a scathing glance over her, leaving her in no doubt about his feelings.

She barely managed to catch her answering snarl in time. Prime directive? What the fuck...? Did he think they were in some episode of *Star Trek*?

"Subjects?" Voice light, she gave him a poker face to look at again. She only just managed it, the air around her virtually humming with her anger. "I thought the politically correct term was patients."

Fitzgerald's eye started to twitch at the corner, a reddish purple flush blooming over his skin like a sunrise over the desert. Antonia didn't drop her gaze like a good little minion. Just watched as the red turned redder and a wave of purple washed down his neck.

His heart pounded out a furious and angry beat as his blood pressure rose, the heat of the red fluid within the thin casing between it and her fangs a siren's call. Perhaps he'd do them all a favor and burst something critical. If that happened, all operations would be off. The cleanup would be shunted to another facility, the RAs wouldn't be needed and Garry would be off the hook.

Just long enough for her to get him the hell out of here.

As she watched, Fitzgerald got it together. Rolling his neck, he closed his eyes for a second. A whiff of emotion-laden sweat assaulted her nostrils as he pulled at his uniform collar.

He opened his eyes to look directly at her, and Antonia read her own death in his eyes. Maybe not today, or tomorrow, but sometime soon he'd find a way to have her killed.

This time for good.

"Remember your place, Major."

This time his voice was calm as he turned back to the window. Lifting a hand, he flicked an intercom switch next to the glass.

"Start the procedure."

She stood, frozen into place, as she watched the machinery in cradles on the ceiling swing into action. The virus delivery machinery. She'd seen it before, but in the Bloods area there was one machine per room rather than the whole-scale factory production line here.

At the first whir of machinery, Garry's head whipped around. Craning back, he watched as the delivery units rolled forward on the tracks. He paled, a wordless moan of terror streaming from his lips. Eyes wide with panic, he bucked and fought in the restraints as the unit crawled ever nearer. All around him the blank-eyed prisoners stared unseeing at the ceiling above.

Antonia curled her hands into fists at her sides, nails biting into her toughened palms. She couldn't let them do this...couldn't let them infect him for no reason.

Half turning, she caught the eye of the guard at the back of the room. Instead of watching the room below, he held her gaze. One forefinger tapped his holstered pistol pointedly. The message was horribly obvious. Suck it up, or deal with a hollow point.

She turned back to the window, ignoring the colonel next to her, and forced herself to watch as the one person she counted as something approaching a friend was killed. Murdered.

His fighting didn't achieve anything. The gurney didn't move. Exhausted, he stopped, eyes wide and pupils dilated as the unit trundled into place above him. It stopped with a click. As the needle started to descend, a dark stain spread over his pants at the groin.

"Awwww, bless him," Fitzgerald mocked. "So scared of the widdle needle he pissed his pants."

She grit her teeth so hard she was surprised they didn't break. Fitz was a dead man. She didn't know how, when or where, but she would make sure of it. And, his death wouldn't be an easy one.

The needle reached the end of its track. Garry closed his eyes. Antonia refused to. She refused to do him the dishonor of turning away.

Fluid built up on the tip of the needle, and grew until it was a greenish-black ball. It fell. Garry flinched as it hit his cheek, making a little splash-mark.

Go easy my friend, and rest assured you will be avenged.

He gasped as the fluid disappeared into his skin. She knew how virulent the RA-17 virus could be, but even Antonia was surprised at how swiftly it killed. With seconds the room filled with gasping as Garry and those around him fought for breath with lungs no longer able to process oxygen. They spasmed, backs arching and heels drumming. One after the other, they slumped lifeless to the gurneys.

Dead. For now.

If nothing else the Project was an efficient machine. Within minutes of Antonia leaving Operations, a transport convoy was being assembled. Already in combat uniform, she made a quick trip back to her room for her tactical-rig.

"Fuck!"

Once inside the relative privacy of her room, she released the tumult of emotions warring inside her. She slammed her fist into one of the rooms support columns. Her head and shoulders were showered with powdered concrete from the force of the blow.

They'd killed him. They'd killed Garry. All for talking to her. Fitzgerald was a dead man. She'd kill him slowly…tear his throat out and lap the blood up as he watched her with dying eyes. Or tear his intestines out through his ass, just to watch him whimper and scream like a little girl. She wrinkled her nose. No, scratch that last. She wanted nothing to do with that man's ass.

A heavy sigh on her lips she pushed away from the column. Right now she couldn't afford wet dreams of killing that sniveling little bastard. She had a job to do. Her last. Then she was coming back and going on a hunt—for a full-bird colonel.

She left the room completely in control. On the surface, anyway. Her tac-rig slung over her shoulder and rifle in her arms, she returned to the transport area to find the RA crate already loaded.

Coming to a stop next to the transport officer, she looked around the assembled vehicles.

"How we doing for time?"

He looked up with a start. "Huh? Oh, sorry, Major, I didn't see you there. We're good. The payload is already strapped down. We're just waiting on a driver, and then you're hot to trot."

She nodded. "I'll wait in the cab."

Chapter Seven

"C-clean up team?"

Hating the slight shake in her voice, Lillian followed Jack down the corridor. She tried not to look at the bodies on the floor. Faces stretched into hideous screams, their sightless eyes stared at the ceiling, and their backs were distorted into hideous shapes. A tide of nausea rose to burn the back of her throat. They must have suffered so much pain.

"What happened to them? How did you ki...um, how did they die?"

She fired questions at him as she skirted around the corpses. Her first thought as a member of hospital staff—hell, as a member of the human race—was to try and help them. Something, a survival instinct perhaps, warned her not to mess with things she didn't understand.

She pulled her foot back, making sure not to touch the ever-widening pool of blood. It was thick as tar, and her gut told her it was dangerous.

"The second guard hardly has a scratch on him. How did you...what did you do to him? Just what the hell is going on?" she asked as she scurried after him.

His long strides ate up the corridor. She tried like hell not to ogle his backside, still playing peek-a-boo through the flaps of the gown. How was a girl supposed to think with prime male flesh like that on display? Unbidden an image rose in her mind. Those firm ass cheeks clenching and relaxing as he drove into her…

Color burned her cheeks as she banished the image. What *was* going on with her? She felt like she'd been dropped into a cross between *The Twilight Zone* and a bad horror movie, surrounded by corpses, and she couldn't stop ogling Jack. She couldn't lust after him, not at the moment. It was entirely inappropriate. Maybe if they'd met outside the hospital… No, she shook her head to herself. That still wouldn't work. He looked liked a model straight out of one of the glossy magazines from the waiting room. She might have admired him from the other side of a bar, but she'd never have plucked up the courage to approach him.

"I didn't do anything to them. The Project did." His lips pressed together as he stopped in front of one of the secure cells and studied the lock for a second.

"They create us in controlled conditions. They don't want random infections and creatures like me on the loose. So they pump their people full of shit to make sure it doesn't happen." He nodded back toward the twisted corpses. "That happens instead."

He looked back at the door. His strong fingers traced the shape of the lock, as though caressing the metal. "Are these double or triple locked?"

"Just double. Hey no, you can't—" she protested, reaching out to warn him. The secure cells housed the most dangerous patients. *Oh yeah,* the little voice in her head sneered, *more dangerous than a guy who grows claws and slices bits off people?*

Too late. He drew his arm back. Claws glinted in the dull light as he slashed at the locks. Metal screamed and parted, cut through as cleanly as though he'd taken a laser-cutter to the door.

Lillian's jaw dropped. Cutting someone's hand off was hard, but she knew how fragile the human body could be, how little force it took to damage it beyond repair. But cutting through a solid steel reinforced door was something else entirely.

"What are you...Wolverine?"

His lips quirked as he slid her a look. The amber leeched back into his eyes again. The sight took her breath away. She was beginning to realize that meant the thing inside him was beginning to emerge.

"Yeah. Something like that. Better looking, though." He threw her a wink.

She snorted. Men, all ego.

"Yeah, right. Sure you are."

"Stay here."

He yanked the door open and disappeared into the cell. Stunned, she didn't argue. She jumped and snatched her hand back from the door. The cut mechanisms within lost their balance and tumbled down within the metal frame with a loud clatter.

Worried, she glanced quickly up the corridor. *Someone had to have heard that.* Any minute now the rest of the military guards would be hot-footing it down the corridor.

She needn't have worried. Snarls erupted from the cell, drowning out the small noise she'd made and creating even more noise. Her heart slammed into her chest again, setting up a frantic rhythm as the sounds of a struggle reached her ears.

Wheels screamed in protest, followed by a metallic thud she recognized as a bed being slammed against a wall. Over it all was an angry snarling that increased in volume and malevolence. A meaty smack reached her ears, quickly followed by a yelp.

Not caring about what she'd been told, she shoved the door open. The windows on this wing were all barred, but that only stopped the inmates escaping. It didn't stop moonlight streaming in as strong as the light of day.

Like a spotlight, it picked out the two men in the middle of the room. Jack, grim-faced determination etched into every line of his large body, had another heavily built guy in a chokehold.

She gasped, her hand flying to her throat. The man stiffened, his head thrown back as he howled. As she watched in horror, his body changed shape. The sounds of bones popping and cracking filled the cell as his knee joints switched direction, stretching the skin around them in a sickening display. If she didn't know better, she'd think she was on the set of a horror film.

A sense of the surreal and insane surrounded her. She fought the giggle as it tried to escape her lips. Only last week she'd complained to her friends about her boring life. Right now, with a patient claiming to be a werewolf, she'd be quite happy with boredom. After this lot, sanity would be an optional extra.

Within seconds, the hideous sounds stopped and his knees finally decided which direction they wanted to face. He went from sagging against Jack, with his head bowed, to straightening up until he stood on his own two feet. Finally he lifted his head, looking through the dark curtains of shoulder-length hair, and she gasped.

He had the same strange amber eyes as Jack when he was...not fully human. Unlike Jack's eyes, these were not warm and patient. In this man's eyes, she could clearly see the beast within, and it scared her.

The next few seconds all happened too fast for her to process. One moment the guy was standing next to Jack, the next he lunged for her, hunger and lust in his eyes. She screamed. Back-pedaled fast. Her ass hit the door, and she went down hard, her feet scrambling uselessly against the floor as she tried to get away.

He was almost on her, his breath hot as it fanned against her neck and the big bulk of his body looming over her. She tensed and turned away. Any moment now, the same vicious claws as Jack's would tear into her soft flesh. He was too fast, she couldn't fight, and she couldn't move fast enough to get away. Her legs shook, fear making her weak and heightening all her senses. Her heart thundered in her chest yet over it she could hear the *tick-tock* of the clock in the hallway as it marked the seconds to her death.

Seconds stretched out into years, but the blow didn't come. Instead there was a yelp. The angry presence and hot breath over her disappeared. Yanked away with the skitter of claws on the linoleum.

"No." Jack's voice was as sharp and scolding as if he were speaking to a misbehaving puppy. "Mine."

Jack watched with careful eyes as Darce fought for control on the floor. Flat on his back, with a large arm over his eyes, the big man's broad chest heaved as he dragged air into his lungs.

"Darce…you cool, man?"

Jack couldn't see his eyes, but they weren't the only clues as to what Darce would do next. He moved a step closer to the man on the floor. Every muscle in his body was tense, adrenalin running through him. Any moment he expected the other man to explode into action and try to get to Lilly. Until the silver madness was out of his system, Darce would be unpredictable. He always was.

The moon disappeared behind a cloud, and the glow streaming through the windows cut by half. Jack held his breath. He was an Alpha, the lead wolf in the section. He was faster, stronger and more powerful than the rest of them. Even a little moonlight had enabled him to burn through the drugs that held him prisoner. The others had to work more at it, a process that could rob them of human reason for a while.

"Darce...?"

Crap. He was going to have a fight on his hands if Darce couldn't break through. He knew he could take the other man. He'd always been able to best any of his men in combat, both when they'd been human and now, when they weren't. But it was the last thing he needed, with Walker setting off the alarm and a suppression team about to breathe down their necks.

"Come on, man, fight it. I need you fit and thinking human. Walker set the alarm. Forget the shit hitting the fan, this place is gonna look like Armageddon soon."

Darce shuddered. His spine arched into a hard bow as his heels drummed the floor in a rapid tattoo. Even in the half-light that rendered everything in shades of gray, Jack could see the beads of silver as they poked out his pores.

He moved, slid to his knees next to his second in command. Grabbing his hand, Jack held it tight. "That's it, man. Push the bastard stuff out. You can do it."

The silver beads grew in size as Darce fought his own body, until it looked as if the soldier had a serious thing about piercings. The chemical scent hit Jack's sensitive nose like a freight train. His wolf went wild, trying to get away from the stench. Gritting his teeth, he forced it into submission.

He would to pay for it later, but he didn't care. His

relationship with the thing inside him was symbiotic, rather than parasitic as he'd believed at first. He got increased speed, strength and the ability to shrug off wounds that would kill a normal man. In return, all his wolf wanted was to run free.

Darce nodded, grabbing Jack's hand in his as he fought to expel the silver. The beads grew until they couldn't maintain their shape. One by one they fell, the silver leaving a black trail in its wake as they rolled down his cheeks.

"Can I help?" The soft voice behind Jack made them both jump. Holy shit. He'd forgotten Lilly was in the room. The last thing he needed was a woman added to the mix, not while Darce was so volatile.

"Lilly, into the corridor," he warned as he prepared to hold Darce down.

A tiny noise from below him made him look down. Darce's eyes were open. Silver pooled on the floor beneath the other man, and his face was streaked with black, but his eyes were human brown.

"I got it, Cap'n. Thinking human."

Relief flooded through Jack, and he switched his grip to haul Darce to his feet.

"Lilly, I'd like you to meet my right hand man. Lieutenant Darcy Foster. Apart from the fact he has a girls name, he's not half bad as a soldier."

The woman was beautiful. For a moment Darce couldn't speak, struck dumb in awe. He breathed in, careful not to draw attention to himself, and rolled her scent over his tongue. She even smelled fantastic. A floral, exotic fragrance clung to the surface of her skin, swaths of it releasing into the air every time she moved. He recognized it, or at least part of it...the low-level musk that every wolf yearned to smell.

She was a wolf-mate.

It was different for every one of them. Any Lycan could tell she was destined to bond with one of them, but her scent would only resonate on a soul-deep level with her destined mate. Under the influence of silver, he'd smelled the mate-scent and reacted instinctively, thinking she was to be his. Now himself again, he recognized the scent wasn't quite right.

Darce's gaze locked onto the woman again. He knew he was staring, but quite frankly, he didn't care.

Forget beautiful, she was gorgeous. Petite and with the sort of full curves any straight red-blooded male would kill to get his hands on. The wolf-mate scent clinging to her skin was just the icing on the "want now" cake.

She wasn't his. Her scent wasn't right and besides, the way the captain hovered around her—managing to roll protective and possessive into one potentially violent package—her chosen mate had already found her.

He smiled as she approached, careful to keep his grin human, even though his wolf was still too close to the surface for comfort. His fangs ached, lying in wait just behind his blunt human teeth.

Jack was less than a step behind her. His gaze, more amber than blue, locked onto Darce's outstretched hand as though it were a poisonous snake. He didn't blame the guy.

Darce wasn't the pack alpha, but he was next in line, and he could change almost as quickly as Jack could. He'd even begun to master the partial shifts, changing just his hands and leaving everything else human, something only the most powerful of them could manage.

He didn't blame Jack for being protective, not when the hand he'd extended to Lillian could sprout claws at any moment. The merest scratch would infect a normal human, and the mating-scent would only make her more susceptible. He had no doubt that if he even looked at the cute brunette askance, Jack would take more than a pound of flesh as a punishment.

“Hi. I think it’s a nice name. Unusual but nice.” She smiled shyly as she put her hand in his and shook gently. “I’m Lillian Rosewood. I’m...one of the staff here. I take it you already know Jack?”

One of the staff? Darce’s grip on her hand tightened for a second. Like the rest of the pack, he had no reason to like and every reason to hate doctors.

Her face whitened, and her lips compressed as she carefully tried to extricate her hand. Jack stepped forward, an unmistakable snarl of anger on his lips. Belatedly, Darce realized he was crushing her hand and dropped it.

“Sorry. Don’t know my own strength at times. And thanks, I kinda like it.”

He added a charming smile to ease the tension and backed off a step. The last thing he needed after pushing what felt like a boatload of silver through his pores was a fight with Jack. He might have almost mastered a part-shift, but Jack was pack alpha, and a master of the shift. He was so adept, the guy could shift just his fingernails into lethal, three-inch talons. Mad shifting skills the rest of them could only talk about in envy.

“So...you’re a doctor here?” he asked carefully, shooting a quick look at Jack. The Project were real careful about outsiders knowing what they were up to, and even more careful about other medical staff getting a looksee at their “people”.

If Lillian was a doctor, and she knew what they were...then Jack had just signed her death warrant. Hell, even if she wasn’t a doctor and knew, the Project wouldn’t allow her to live. His eyes unfocused as a wave of the mating scent hit him again and threatened to short-circuit his brain. If she was a wolf-mate, and Jack's mate, then the pack would be obligated to keep her safe.

She smiled. "Oh, no. No, I'm not. I'm the hospital manager."

"Fuck me sideways," he breathed, understanding in his eyes as he looked at Jack. He wouldn't want to be the guy's shoes for all the money in the world now. He'd gone from having nothing to live for, to having everything to live for...and everything to protect against an enemy who would stop at nothing to achieve its aim.

"I'd rather not. Why, what's wrong...you got a thing against admin staff?"

"Huh? What?"

Her swift retort surprised him, and the sly humor in her eyes made him smile again. Catching Jack's warning glare, he made himself pay better attention, but not too much, to the lady he spoke with.

"No, not at all, pretty lady. I was just thinking we should count our lucky stars. Help on tap with all the horrendous report forms they make us fill out. In blood," he wailed dramatically, hand over his heart. He peeked out from under the heavy fall of his hair and winked at her.

Jack's lips compressed, and he all but shoved his petite mate behind him. "That's quite enough of that, we need to find the others and formulate a plan. Walker triggered a remote alarm. We're gonna get company and soon."

Darce nodded, and snapped back to the seasoned and experienced soldier he was. "On it boss-man. You keep the little lady safe, and I'll round up the lads."

Chapter Eight

Less than an hour later, Lilly was surrounded by grim-faced men and one woman in the staff break room of the military wing. She should have been comforted by the presence of a woman among them, but somehow the strange ice-blue stare of Private Nicole Smith disconcerted her. Especially after she and another of the team had been dispatched to deal with the rest of the guards. The terror in the screams that had echoed through the corridors was something she never wanted to hear again.

"Right, these are the plans of the hospital. Lilly tells me non-military patients are minimal at the moment. Apart from us, St. Mary's is an open facility. Most patients are allowed home visits, so they're offsite for the weekend."

Nic snorted in bitter amusement. "Christ, the madmen really do run the asylum. But that means less for us to worry about. Think they'll use blood-suckers or re-animates?"

Lilly edged closer to Jack, her single source of comfort and security in a world gone mad. He'd lost the hospital gown, as had all the people clustered around the table someone had dragged into the center of the room.

They were dressed in a combination of combat pants and jeans, and most were barefoot. One blond guy—Lilly couldn't remember his name—had a pair of pink sneakers on. All were naked to the waist, except Nic, who was wearing a tank top with a smiley face on it. Apart from the single, slender female among them, the amount of ripped male flesh on display made Lillian feel a little lightheaded.

"Re-animates for sure. They can't risk us turning the Bloods. They haven't figured out the inoculations to stop cross infection yet. And we still have some patients and staff to worry about. They're holed up in the other wing at the moment."

The conversation made her head whirl. Most of it she couldn't follow. Military-sounding words she'd never heard before and had no idea what they meant. Other words made her shiver, a part of her brain not *wanting* to know what they meant.

They didn't look like soldiers, not the way they dressed, anyway. They looked more like models. Although she'd thought him too young to have signed up, Jack was older than the rest. His hair was close-cropped. The rest had more hair than the average surfer, flowing down to their shoulders in a shaggy mess. It didn't look like a conscious decision kind of style as much as a "let it do its own thing" kind.

They were soldiers, though; that much was evident in the way they crowded around the table in an impromptu war council. And the small tattoo each had on their rib cage said far more than any talk of tactics.

She shivered. She'd seen them before. Meat tags. Which meant they were from a unit that went into extreme action, into combat so violent that bodies were rarely found whole.

"Ugh..." The groan started by Nic echoed around the table. "I freaking *hate* RAs! They taste bad."

Lillian frowned. Tasted bad? She opened her mouth, but shut it again with a click. She didn't want to know. She *really* didn't want to know.

Thump…thump…thump.

The sudden noise outside made her jump. Before she could react, light stabbed through the windows, constantly moving and searching, as though a giant shone a torch inside to look for something.

Nic pushed the office chair she sat astride back and rolled toward the window. Leaning against the windowsill she looked up, craning her neck. “Two choppers with spots. Two more behind them, look like gunships.”

Jack nodded. “Clean-up. We have about ten before the transports arrive.”

Tension spiked sharply, as though it had barged through the door and filled up all the available space to watch proceedings. Jack looked around the grim-faced group.

“Okay, the terrain’s too open to make a break for it yet, not with those gunships out there. All we can do is lock down tight and sit through the first wave. Once the re-animates are in position, the ships should peel off.”

Darce nodded, leaning forward eagerly. “Then we spilt? The RAs aren’t fast enough to keep up with us. Not when we’re shifted and hot-footing it.”

Jack shook his head.

“Nope, we can’t leave this place undefended. RAs are dumb, but they’ll easily get into the other wing. You want innocent blood on our hands? Even if they are crazy, no one deserves that.”

He spread out the floor plan of the hospital Lillian had given him earlier. The paper crackled as he flattened it down. When the new extension for the therapy pool had been built, the architects had done a full work up on the whole building. She’d no idea why she’d kept it, but now she was glad she had. Jack’s eyes had lit up when she’d pulled it from the cupboard in her office.

"We've all fought RAs before, so this should be a walk in the park. Yeah, they're strong as fuck and go down fighting, but they're as thick as shit. If we lock down all these corridors here and here, and open these and the front door, we can create a killing field here with cross fire."

He tapped the middle of the map, over an area that displayed where four corridors intersected in a staggered cross. The secondary branches were off to the secure wards, which meant they had a dual steel gate system not unlike an airlock. But instead of air, this one was designed to stop patients getting out. Or anything else getting in.

"Any that get through that will face Darce, Sanders and Nic. Any questions?" He looked up and around the group but no one replied. "Thom and Nic, you get down and unlock the front doors. Darce, go with them for cover fire, then get your ass back here. Everyone else, positions."

The group around the table scattered, all going their own ways. Once they were alone Jack rounded the table and approached her where she was curled up on the single couch.

"Hey sweetheart, how you hanging in there?"

He crouched down in front of her, the heavy muscles of his chest and torso doing an intricate two-step as he reached out and took both her hands in his.

"Other than I have no clue what's going on and feel like I've been plunged into an episode of *The Twilight Zone*, then yeah, I'm peachy. Thanks for asking."

She knew she was being snarky, but she didn't much care. She'd been pulled from pillar to post, seen men die hideously and she was supposed to believe that Jack and his men were some kind of military-created Lycanthropes.

Werewolves in St. Mary's? It sounded like the title of a

cheesy B-movie and was so ludicrous she wanted to laugh. She suspected if she started now, though, she'd never stop. If she hadn't seen those wicked claws herself...she shook her head. Perhaps she was seeing things, a trick of the light. Yeah, that must be it. Otherwise she was going nuts. *In a mental institution. How fitting.*

"Okay, time out. I get the werewolves, but what the *fuck* are RAs? And Bloods?"

Jack suppressed his sigh. He didn't have time for this right now, but the suspicious shine in Lillian's eyes, and the barely restrained hysteria within, told him that he'd better make time. Cursing, he marshaled his thoughts to put everything in an order she could understand. Maybe. At least he hoped so.

Normally, the project took its time prepping new recruits and staff. From the barrage of tests, through to the numerous friendly "chats" with the facility counselor, by the time the truth was laid on out there on the line, each newbie had been well prepared. Less likely to have an unstable moment.

The whole initiation process should take weeks, but he had to accomplish it in minutes. With a woman who was already half terrified.

"Okay, here goes. The Project is a secret organization operating within the Army. They're government backed but I don't know how far up the chain of command they go."

Her eyebrow winged up, but he forged on anyway.

"They take people like me, pump them full of something...something that changes us. All I know is that I went in human and I came out like this...with this thing inside me. They control us, with more drugs and threats. If we rebel, we end up places like this, or worse. Silver bullet to the back of the head and an unmarked grave somewhere."

He dropped his gaze, watching his thumb as he ran it over the back of her hand. She was tiny, her bones delicate under her skin. Beside her he felt huge, like a brute. He...the creature inside him...could hurt her so easily. His wolf wouldn't hurt her, though. The damn thing was more likely to roll over and let her rub his tummy.

"We're only one branch of research. There're Bloods and the re-animates as well..."

"Whoa, whoa. In English, please."

She turned her hands and laced her slender fingers through his larger callused ones. He wrapped his fingers around hers, desperate for the touch of her skin.

"You mentioned those earlier. If you tell me Bloods mean vampires, I *will* decide you're crazy and walk out."

"Okay," he agreed amiably.

Silence stretched between them for a long moment. The penny dropped and her jaw went suddenly slack.

"Shit. You're not kidding, are you? So if the Bloods are vampires, then what are the re-animates? No, don't tell me...they're zombies!"

She was being facetious, but Jack couldn't help smiling. Quickly he smothered the expression and looked at her seriously.

"Sorry babe, but you got it in one."

"Jesus fucking Christ." She ran a shaking hand through her hair. "Okay, say I believe you and somehow I've dropped into some kind of *Resident Evil* inspired nightmare...what happens now?"

If he could have kept the next words to himself, he would have. Blunt and forthright, he'd never been one to mince his words. He called a spade a spade. One part of him wanted not to tell her, to gather her in his arms and make a run for it so she didn't have to deal with the horror the night was about to become.

If he did that, he could take her over the mountains. Find a town and let her go... As soon as the thought entered his mind, his wolf sat up and took notice. The thing didn't bother much with his human thoughts, but the very idea of letting Lillian go, never seeing her again, had his wolf snarling a warning at him.

"We go down with the others. The re-an...the zombies come in. We kill them in a variety of bloody and gruesome ways. We try and stay alive until they're all dead or the sun comes up. They're slow in the sunlight. We can make a break for the mountains then. With us gone, the Project will leave this place alone and the people...your patients and staff...will be safe."

She nodded. He could feel the question hanging between them. "What about me?" shone clearly in her chocolate, puppy-dog eyes. He ignored it, letting go of her hands to clap his own on his thighs and stand.

"Your choice, Lillian. You can go hide with the others in the secure wing. Or you can come with me, and see what the government is hiding from you."

Chapter Nine

The gates of St. Mary's were old and imposing. For many years, they had been a symbol of care and treatment for those in society deemed too unstable to deal with reality. Austere yet welcoming, they never closed. Any man, woman or child could walk through those gates and take the long walk up to the hospital set on the hill, and be sure of help once they reached their destination.

It was calm, peaceful. Tranquil.

That silence shattered as military helicopters screamed through the air toward them, so low that the backwash from their blades whipped the vegetation on either side of the old iron gates into a frenzy. Spotlights snapped on, trained onto the hospital on the hill.

The trap was sprung. Clean-up had arrived.

Within seconds, the ground rumbled, the sound growing in strength until heavy military transporters turned the corner. They rolled toward the gates, an unstoppable force. Metal squealed against stone as the first cut a deep grove into the gate's stone support, leaving a wound of bright cream stone against the weather-beaten exterior.

The gates wobbled.

The second vehicle turned in, catching the damaged stone column as it passed. The stone swayed, wobbled. Finally, with the elegant surrender of a bygone era, it collapsed.

The gates of St. Mary's fell.

"Jeez! Just *try* to be a little more careful, would ya?" Antonia snapped as the transporter rocked and rolled like a boat on the high seas. In the rear-view mirror, the stone wall toppled into the road, making the vehicle behind them swerve. It was that or half a ton of rock on the hood, something that would put a serious crimp in anyone's day.

"Remember, we have a live payload. There's no way I want to try and round up a dozen hungry RAs and stuff them back in Pandora's box. Do you?" she directed at the young driver.

One of the new troops into camp, he was so young she'd have been surprised if he had to shave yet. And no one could miss the sparkle of interest in his eyes as he looked at her.

"I can handle anything, doll." He winked at her as he swung the big vehicle around and onto the long drive up the hill toward the hospital. The muscles in his arms stood in high relief as he fought the steering wheel. "Seen it, done it and got the T-shirt to prove it."

Despite herself, Antonia's lips quirked. He was cute, very cute, but human. Which meant that if the things in the container behind them got out, he had a life expectancy of less than nine seconds.

Thinking of the container reminded her of what had happened the last time she got even marginally friendly with one of the human staff. Wiping the smile from her lips, she shot him a "don't fuck with me" glare.

"Just be more careful. And it's *Major*, not 'doll'. Comprende?"

"Yes, sir! Sorry, sir. Won't happen again, sir," he replied briskly, snapping his eyes front and center.

She had to give it to him, he was *way* more intelligent than Fitzgerald. That guy wouldn't get a hint if you put it in a truck and ran him over with it.

"Good."

They trundled up the last incline, and the hospital suddenly stood in front of them. She shifted in her seat, leaning forward and looking up so she could see all of it. Four stories, it was an immense building, especially for this area. Imposing and dramatic, it stood on the hill in defiance of the elements and the desert fast encroaching from the west.

She tapped the discreet plug in her ear and started a running commentary to help with her report later. "Lights out, looks like the main power's already offline."

Thwap-thwap-thwap. The sound of chopper blades overhead was accompanied by a dust storm, and the transport was bathed in bright white light.

"Gunships already onsite. Quarantine lines already in place."

Opening her door, she stood on the first step and waved the chopper off. The turbulence from its blades whipped her hair into a frenzy around her face but she ignored it in favor of looking over the target location.

"Main reception looks all quiet—"

The flutter of movement tugged at the corner of her eye. Instantly she zeroed in on it, her eyes as sharp as a hawk.

"Movement, second floor. Looks like one of the hospital staff. Yeah, more people at the window. Not a threat. Get the secondary team around the other side and start the evacuation," she ordered as she turned her attention back to the main entrance and ignored the civilians—hospital staff and patients alike—who were staring down at the military convoy in a mixture of fascination and fear.

The other wing and the main reception area were both dark. No movement at all. Her instincts told her that was where their problem would be. Nothing Lycans liked more than a dark hole to skulk in. Damn creatures loved to hide or ambush their prey. She hissed through her teeth as she folded herself back into the cab.

"Okay, swing around and back up to the entrance. When we drop the tail gate, I don't want any of these fuckers getting loose," she ordered, her voice sharp and no-nonsense. "Because if that happens, I'll be burning more than a bunch of dogs and RAs here tonight."

The courtyard at the front of the hospital exploded into a hive of activity. As the transporter started to back up, the other vehicles surrounded the area. A cordon of steel completed by commandos with enough weaponry to arm a small regiment. Their grim faces were all locked on the main entrances and the large transporter between them and it. She wasn't sure which they were more wary of...the Lycans within the building or the RAs they were sending in to deal with them.

Shaking her head, she looked back at the entrance and started. The door stood open. Half a second later, the commandos registered the change as well and a host of rifles were aimed at the black gap within.

Winding her window down, her arm pumping in swift, circular motions, she bellowed, "Hold your fire!"

"Just hold it here for a second," she told the driver next to her, and studied the door with a frown on her face. *Why had they opened the door? What was the point?* It was as if they were inviting entry, even though they had to know what the Project would send in after them.

Not much could kill a Lycan. A Blood could, and vice versa, but cross-infection was deemed too much of a risk. She'd only ever heard one whispered tale of it around the camp, and the story claimed that the subject had been eliminated instantly. If it was true, she didn't blame them. Such a creature would be too powerful for even the Project to contain.

RAs couldn't be re-infected by anything. Once the RA17 virus had taken hold, they were literally walking, rotting corpses. She shuddered again. While it was a nasty way to go, at least they weren't aware. The initial reaction to the serum killed off most autonomic and all higher mental functions. For most anyway—the scientists had theorized that some subjects retained self-awareness, but at the first hint of it, they'd been put down and the serum adjusted. Since then they'd had no problems.

Something moved in the rectangle of darkness set into the pale stone of the building. She squinted, her enhanced eyesight struggling to bring whatever it was into focus.

It was a man. He stepped forward a little, just into her range of vision but still shrouded by darkness and unseen by the humans around her.

A Lycan. He was in human form, but she still knew what he was. His eyes burned with amber fire. Instinctively, her lips curled back from her fangs as her gaze riveted on him. He was possibly the most handsome man she'd ever seen. Even with the unnatural amber hue to his eyes, he was gorgeous. Everything feminine in her responded, even as her Blood instincts yammered at her to rip the door open, race across the distance that separated them and destroy him.

As though he could sense her internal struggle, he grinned, winked and blew her a kiss. Then he was gone, swallowed up by the darkness so even her Blood-enhanced eyes could no longer see him.

"Crap!"

"What? What did you see?" The driver asked, leaning against the steering wheel as he tried to look around her.

Without a word, she leaned back so his view was unimpeded. Air whistled between his teeth.

"Fuck. They opened the front door."

"Bring it around. That's it...back up, back up. Further...you could get a damn tank through there. Where'd you learn to drive...a go-cart track?"

A tense half hour later the stream of abuse from the soldier guiding the transporter back toward the now open door of the hospital was constant and scathing. Standing to one side, rifle held loosely in her hands, Antonia ignored it. It was just banter, the same the world over...get a group of soldiers in one place, and within two minutes they'd start insulting one another. Guaranteed.

"At least I *can* drive. You suck at it."

She sighed and started to count, her eyes still on the open door. The darkness beyond was empty. The Lycan had gone. She knew that, and she knew that shortly they'd release the RAs to go hunt him and his friends down. Death by mindless cadaver. Hell of a way to go. So why did she feel like running in there and warning him?

"That's not what your mom said when I was climbing off her this morning..."

And there it was. The "your mom" joke. Shaking her head, Antonia stepped forward. "If you're all finished...let's get this show on the road, shall we?"

There were rumblings and disgruntled expressions, but the chatter cut to a minimum as the transporter rolled the last couple of feet back toward the door and ground to a halt in a hiss of air-brakes. Silence settled for a second. The call had come through from the other team to confirm the hospital was empty of civilians. Which meant it was showtime.

"Lock and load, people!" she yelled as she looped her rifle across her back out of the way and started to undo the heavy bolts and deadlocks on the back of the transporter.

"Keep eyes on that door and stay back. Cutting loose the RAs!"

She jumped back on her last words, narrowly avoiding being clipped by the heavy metal of the ramp as it swung down. The edge slammed into the ground, the impact lifting a cloud of dirt and chipping the worn flagstones. After today, the courtyard would be the least of the hospital's worries. They'd be more concerned with the wing she was about to burn down to contain the Lycan infection.

Grabbing the door strap from the side of the container, she wrapped it around her wrist and took three running steps. On the last, she swung herself into the air, using her body weight and momentum to open the metal door, all that was left between the RAs and freedom.

It squealed as it swung open. The low-level moaning they'd all been ignoring grew louder. Not the sound of a creature in pain, nor could it be likened to the noise cattle made. It was dull and monotonous, like the air escaping from a set of moth-eaten bagpipes with rotten insides. A broken sound, an unnatural sound, and it was getting louder.

Her feet hit the ground the other side of the vehicle, and she looped the restraining strap into the hook made for it.

"Perkins and Fletcher, get your asses front and center," she yelled, but the two flame-thrower operatives were already moving. One on each side, they flanked the vehicle, tanks primed and pilot lights lit. Perkins on the left ignited and a stream of flame lit the courtyard up in shades of orange and yellow, restoring the colors of daytime for a few seconds.

She swung her gaze to Fletcher and waited for him to test his flame. Flame-throwers were the best defense against the RAs, but they were notoriously temperamental. Her brow furrowed as the dry *click-click-click* of Fletcher pulling the trigger reached her ears.

Something heavy thudded against the side of the container. The moaning intensified, enriched by the sound of shuffling feet. One eye on the ramp and the other on Fletcher, Antonia held her breath. He needed to get that flame to catch, and soon. Within seconds. The RAs might be the modern, real-life equivalent of zombies, but that didn't mean they were the shuffling snail-like creatures of moviedom. Once they'd got a whiff of live meat, those fuckers were *fast.*

The first RA appeared at the top of the ramp. On a passing glance, he looked normal. As normal as any of the RA stock looked, anyway. Straight from the cells, with buzz-cut hair, he modeled the latest line in prison-orange jumpsuits.

Pausing, he swung his head from left to right, as though looking for something. There was no spark of vitality in his eyes, his jaw slack. A thin line of drool connected his lips to his shoulder. Even in this light Antonia could see his skin was the green-gray of approaching decay, the veins within black with corrupt blood.

"Light the damn flame," she muttered between gritted teeth, even though Fletcher was too far away to hear. It didn't matter, the tight look on his face and his controlled movements all broadcast that he knew the clock was ticking.

Click-click-click.

Crap. The thrower wouldn't catch. As unobtrusively as she

could, she moved toward Fletcher, her rifle at the ready. Dully, the re-animate on the ramp turned in her direction, attention caught by her movement. Its eyes didn't focus, but she didn't let that fool her. Already the front of its jumpsuit was soaked with drool and it had begun to chew. Never a good sign.

"Fletch, move back and behind me," she ordered in a low voice, aiming her rifle. The RA's head was dead center in her sights. They might be fast, they might be nigh on impossible to kill, but nothing could operate well after she'd unloaded a full magazine into their skull.

"It'll catch, Major. The pilot's just a bit dicey at times."

The sharp stink of sweat rose to surround her as he pulled the trigger again. The thunder of his heartbeat filled her ears, the fast flow of blood a siren's call to her nonhuman instincts. As always, the darkness inside her uncoiled, presented her with images of feeding... What it would be like to wrap the soldier in her strong arms, bare his neck and sink her fangs deep into his throat.

"Get. Back." Her voice no longer sounded normal, but like a guttural growl, as the RA attacked.

One second it was swaying slightly on the ramp, as though listening to its own internal soundtrack, and the next it charged. Teeth bared and a loud moan of hunger issuing from its lips, it ran down the ramp.

Crap. She had to get the one who hadn't gone into rigor yet. Time stretched out as it ran toward her, its eyes now fixed on Fletcher. Her heart thudded in her chest once, twice, as she tracked him through her sights. She pulled the trigger, first pressure...full.

The courtyard was filled with the sharp retort of automatic gunfire. The RA jerked like a marionette as her shots slammed between his dead eyes. His skull exploded in a shower of bone and splatter of foul brain matter.

Whumph. Beside her, the thrower finally caught and spat a torrent of fire toward the fallen RA.

"Oh yeah, baby! Who's my girl?" Fletcher crowed, relief ringing sharp in his voice. They all knew how close he'd come there.

Eyes sharp, Antonia watched the fallen RA for long moments until she was sure it was down for good. Then she lowered her rifle and nodded at Fletcher.

"Torch it."

He didn't need telling twice. Flame roared as she turned back to the rest. Without a word, they moved back into place. Two of them started to bang on the sides of the container, using the noise to drive the RAs out.

The moaning and shuffling increased, and a group emerged from the darkness onto the ramp. Like a herd of cattle, they moaned...in distress or hunger she couldn't tell...and started down the ramp. None of them showed the speed or predatory instinct of the first one. Instead, they shuffled in a group, all swaying in discordant rhythms and knocking into each other.

Her gaze latched onto the one white-clad figure among the orange. Garry. Her teeth clenched tight as he paused and looked around. Something approaching intelligence entered his dead eyes, as though he were aware she was watching him.

Her heart, ever slow, stalled in her chest. *Please God, no.* He couldn't be aware. They'd said they'd altered the virus to stop any possibility of subject awareness. He couldn't be aware, it would be too cruel, especially considering how terrified he'd been of being infected.

The rest of the group shuffled toward the door, herded by Fletch and Perkins with the throwers. Garry hung back, confusion filtering onto his face like a slow sunrise.

There were shouts behind him as two orange-clad figures broke away from the group. Antonia ignored them, unable to tear her gaze away from her former friend.

"Deal with them," she yelled, as the wayward RAs barreled past Perkins and out the other side of the cordon. "Don't engage, try and herd them through another entrance."

She shook her head. She'd have to deal with these idiots later. Right now, she had more important things to deal with. Frowning, she took a step closer to the RA in front of her.

Awareness had begun to fill his blue eyes, one of them already clouding over with the white film of death. His hands held out in front of him, he looked at them with growing horror.

"Garry?"

He snapped his head up at her voice, focusing on her with effort, and moaned. It was a sound of terror and pure torment. A tear slid down his cheek.

He knew. He was dead and still he knew what they'd done. That they'd turned him into his worst nightmare.

"Huuuu..." he droned, spit leaking from the corner of his lips as he tried to speak. "P-p-puh-puh...peas...pleasssssss..."

He looked at her and held his hands out. Not in the grasping reach she'd seen most RAs use to grab their victims, but instead as if to show her the gray skin and blackened veins.

His eyes held hers. Easily she read the expression in them. They begged her not to leave him like this. Not to let him kill, even though his new nature demanded it. He was...had been...her friend.

Without thinking, she had her rifle in her shoulder, and she looked at his face through her sights. Relief filled his eyes as she pulled the trigger.

The trigger clicked. Nothing happened.

"Fucking *hell!*"

Her magazine was jammed. An unforgivable deadly lapse in a live situation. Swearing, she slung it around her back, pulled her sidearm and aimed square between Garry's eyes. Before she pulled the trigger, she looked directly at him.

"Fitzgerald is a dead man."

Garry nodded and smiled.

She put three bullets through his skull and sent him, finally, to meet his maker.

Chapter Ten

"Fuck me, she shot him."

Safely concealed by darkness and a net curtain on the second floor, Darce watched the little drama play out in the courtyard below. His amber eyes tracked the tall woman as she holstered her pistol. She stood for a long moment, just looking at the body in front of her. That had been real anguish and anger on her face. Definitely a history with whoever the RA had been when he was alive.

Without intervention from his brain, his eyes returned to caress the lines of her slender image. Dressed for combat in black battle fatigues, complete with tac-rig and enough weaponry to give a survival nut a serious hard-on, she was a walking wet dream for a guy like him. Not just for a guy *like* him. For *him*. As he'd opened the main doors, the wind had changed direction for a second and he'd caught a trace of her scent.

The fragrance had hit him broadside, reached deep inside him and stole his ability to breathe right out of his lungs. As soon as he'd caught her scent, he knew. She was the one. Trouble was, she was a Blood. His mate was a heartless, blood-sucking vampire.

Who'd just shot an RA dead…okay, deader…before it could be deployed. As she turned away from the body, something that looked suspiciously like a tear glittered on her cheek. *She was crying? Over killing an RA?* Darce frowned as she walked out of sight, tucking a loose strand of dark hair behind his ear as he moved to try and keep her in view.

"Shit, shit, shit. Come back, pretty lady," he muttered, but she stood too close to the building for him to see. He could *feel* her, as if his body was attuned to her like a compass to true north.

It was no good. She wasn't going to move back into view so he could ogle her some more and, from the sounds he could hear below, the RAs were moving it.

"Later," he promised the unseen beauty below. Blood, or not, she was his, and he *would* claim her.

The corridor was cold and dark. The soldiers outside had cut the power lines, and the backup generator hadn't come online. Since it was in an outbuilding at the rear of the hospital, Lillian suspected that it too had been sabotaged.

Crouched down behind Jack, she tried to creep closer to his warmth without being noticed. Still naked to the waist, he wore a determined expression as he methodically loaded and checked his weaponry. Scattered around him were more weapons. She could only identify the hand pistols, the rest were like something out of an action film. He wasn't alone—one of his men sat against the other wall doing exactly the same. Opposite them, in the other corridor, three other guys were also loading weapons. When done, they'd move back along the twisted corridor so that the two teams weren't shooting directly at each other.

Between them, they had enough guns for a small army.

"Where the hell did you get all those?" she asked, using the question to cover another move closer. She sighed in relief. Warmth rose from his bare skin as if he was some kind of human radiator.

"Guard station on this wing."

Her eyes threatened to bug out of her head. "What? They had all *that* in there?"

He nodded but didn't look at her. He was too busy loading what looked like a hand cannon. She edged closer still, until she was almost leaning against his back, and looked at the small pile.

"Which one do I get?"

His lips compressed. "None of them. You stay behind me and down out of sight behind the cabinet."

She looked at him as though he'd grown another head.

"Excuse me? Can you repeat that? I thought you just told me that I don't get a gun."

He picked up a shotgun and cocked with a swift, efficient movement. "Yup, that's exactly what I said."

"Well, fuck *that!* I want a gun."

"You're not getting one."

He turned his head and favored her with a hard look. Amber leeched into his blue eyes. She glared back. They were at an impasse, one she was determined to win.

"Oh no you don't. Pulling the weird wolf eyes shit on me doesn't work. Now give me a gun. I need one. Hell, after all this weird crap, I damn well *deserve* a way to protect myself."

His eyes were fully amber now, but she didn't back down. She knew him…as much as it was possible to know someone she'd met less than twenty-four hours ago. Instinct told her that neither he nor the creature inside him would harm a hair on her head.

"You talk too much."

"Oh yeah? I can talk more. Especially if it irritates you enough to give me a gun."

Her body tensed, her hands practically itched with the need to grab some form of weaponry. She couldn't sit here knowing something was coming through those doors with no way to defend herself.

"Talk all you want. You're not getting a gun. Have you had any training?" He smirked in triumph when she shook her head. "There, see? You'd only shoot me or, God forbid, yourself if I gave you one."

"Fine."

Lillian sat back on her haunches and crossed her arms as she tried to figure out a way to get him to let her have a gun. Her gaze wandered over to the other soldier with them. He studiously avoided her gaze. Great, so none of them would go up against their almighty alpha.

Refusing to look at the hunk of gorgeousness beside her, she studied the wall of the corridor. Her gaze followed the design in the plaster until...with a grin, she pushed off and marched down the corridor.

"Don't go too far," Jack called out as he continued what he was doing.

Lillian ignored him. She wasn't going far, just to the nearest fire point. Every wing had several of them, each containing different types of extinguishers, a first-aid kit and, locked away safely in a cabinet, a fire axe.

Sliding her jacket off, she wrapped it around her fist and punched the glass.

"Fucking *hell!*"

Pain shot up her arm as her fist connected with the glass.

Glass which remained stubbornly in place and whole. She glared at it as she shook her hand, shoving it under her armpit as she waited for the pain to dissipate. If looks could kill or shatter glass, she'd be fine. But they didn't, so she needed to channel her inner Bruce Lee.

Sighing, she re-wrapped her jacket around her arm and concentrated on the karate moves she'd learned as a kid. Sure, the lessons were nearly twenty years ago, but muscles remembered these things, didn't they?

Taking a deep breath she closed her eyes and moved before she could think about it. Using her elbow, she slammed it against the glass. Her reward was a satisfying crack. The safety glass broke up around her arm, falling harmlessly into the bottom of the cabinet in small cubes.

Crowing with triumph, she reached in and snatched the axe off its bracket. A couple of practice swings only increased the broad grin across her face. Screw Jack, she didn't need his guns. She could arm herself quite nicely, thank you very much.

"Good. You're bac—where the fuck did yo..." Jack paused for a moment to look at the heavy red axe in her hands. He shook his head. "Never mind. We have company."

Darce hit the stairs at a run and thundered down them three at a time. Adrenalin pumping through his body, he raced down the corridor and slid around the last corner and into place between Nic and Sanders. Drunk on the power of his Lycan body and the fact he'd at last scented his true-mate, he grinned at the pair of them.

Sanders lifted an eyebrow but didn't make a comment. Nic looked at him as though he'd grown another head, her ice-blue eyes fixing him with a hard stare. He suppressed a shiver. That was the one thing he would never get used to about Nic's transformation.

Before she'd turned Lycan, her eyes had been the softest green he'd ever seen. The arctic blue was from her wolf. Unlike the rest of the pack, who could play human easily enough if they needed to, Nic's eyes didn't change back to green anymore. He missed her eyes...actually, he missed the softer, laughing Nic he remembered from their days in basic. Then memory smacked him around the back of the head as he recalled his mate outside. He grinned again.

Oh yeah, he felt *good.*

Nic frowned, her gaze flicking over him in assessment as her nose twitched slightly. He'd always found that cute. He'd have reached out and tweaked it...if he didn't know she'd take his arm off at the shoulder for doing it.

She stilled, her expression deadening. Slowly, her gaze marched down to his groin. He didn't bother to hide the tented fabric at his crotch. His scent would give him away anyway.

She lifted her brow, lips pursed. "Impressive. Weird but impressive. Didn't know RAs got you off this badly."

He snorted and waved a hand dismissively. He was in too good a mood to be brought down by her sarcasm.

"She's here!"

He had been going to keep the amazing news to himself, but instead he found himself blurting the words out without any apparent intervention from his brain. Once they were out, there was no taking them back, so he stood in the middle of the corridor grinning like a fool.

The two other wolves froze. There was no question what he meant. A wolf only meant one thing when he said "she" in that tone of voice. He was talking about the other half of his soul, his perfect mate. The woman made especially for him.

"One of the RAs? Man, that sucks. I'm sorry," Sanders, a man of few words, spoke into the silence.

"Oh. God, no. She's not an RA. She's one of the troops that came with them—"

Nic speared him with a look so icy he was surprised his blood didn't freeze. "She? With the troops? There's only one woman with them and she..." Her lip curled in disgust. "She's a Blood."

Darce grinned and nodded like a fool. He knew what she was, and he didn't care.

The female werewolf's gaze stabbed toward his groin again.

"Seriously, Darce? We're about to be overrun by RAs and you've got a boner for some Blood bitch?" Her anger radiated out from her like a porcupines quills. If she'd been in wolf form, her fur would have stood on end. "That's all we need...a new and improved way for them to slaughter us. Send in the hot Blood bitch so you all stop thinking with the big head and follow your dicks around. Fucking heat-seeking missiles!" She shook her head. "Sick, just sick!"

Power filled the corridor. Darce caught his breath as it wandered up his skin, tingling as the pressure grew and grew. It felt like the pressure in a plane cabin as a plane took off. He wriggled his jaw to try and equalize his ears, but before they could, there was a *pop*. Not so much a sound as a feeling against his skin. Where Nic had been standing, there was a two hundred pound white-furred wolf glaring at him in anger instead.

Darce admired her for a moment, careful not to get caught doing it. Nic had a hair-trigger temper and no issues with trying to take down a member of her own squad. Sometimes he wondered where all her rage came from, then he remembered how they'd been made into what they were, and the pieces all fit into place.

If he thought too much about it, all the anger and bitterness locked somewhere deep inside tried to escape and overwhelm him. The difference between him and Nic, hell Nic and most of the squad, was that they didn't let it. They preferred to live in the here and now, and play the hand life had dealt them.

Today, despite the fact they were about to face down a horde of re-animates, Darce felt as if he'd hit the jackpot.

Should he have given her a gun? Jack didn't have long to ponder the question before his sensitive nose got the first whiff of incoming re-animates. His lip curled, even the slightest hint of flesh just starting to rot and blood gone black was enough to curdle his stomach, and set the creature within off.

"RAs inbound," he whispered to the woman at his side. The re-animates were too far away for her to hear yet, and she didn't have the enhanced sense of smell the rest of them had. The low level growl emanating from all around told him the rest of the squad had already picked up the same scents.

Bloods he could deal with. Although they were vicious-fast and liked their food on the rare side, there was at least intelligence there. Some semblance of humanity left. Not much when the bloodlust hit them, but there was some.

Not so with re-animates. They were the zombies Lillian had called them. An experiment into increased regeneration gone wrong, the RA-17 serum had had unexpected and disastrous effects on the test subjects.

It had killed them outright. No argument or confusion. As soon as the serum had been injected it spread through their systems with an ease cyanide would have envied. The subjects had all cocked their toes up there and then, right on the tables. The exact opposite of the intended result.

The bodies zipped up and carted off to the morgue, the experiment had been deemed a failure. Until the next morning. First shift in the morgue had found the night guard, or what remained of him, and five docile, shuffling dead people.

The project scope was quickly altered, and RA-17 was hailed a success. So effective, it was used during cleanup of infection sites. Mortality rates of normal troops against Lycanthropes were high, almost a hundred percent. Those same rates didn't count with re-animates. You couldn't kill something that was already dead.

"What, now? Where?"

Her eyes were wide with a mixture of apprehension and determination. Her knuckles whitened on the shaft of the axe she held. He didn't tell her that he had absolutely no intention of letting her near enough to the RAs for her to use it.

"Side window."

He nodded toward it and checked his weaponry again. Like most soldiers, it was a compulsive need. Move, check weapons. Breathe, check weapons. Fart, check weapons. It was ingrained deep into his psyche.

A shuffling noise reached his ears. The sound of feet dragging against the linoleum. A sound that exasperated the mothers of young children and put Jack and his men on high alert.

Through the window next to them, he looked out across the small grassy area outside to the windows of the corridor that intersected theirs. With all the gates opened, it was the path of least resistance. RAs were dumb, they'd go whichever way they were herded until they couldn't go any farther. After that, everything was up for grabs. If they were left alone, they'd mill about in confusion. If they were stimulated by prey or hungry, they'd kick up a storm.

Indistinct shadows moved behind the barred windows. It could have been a trick of the light, but he knew better. The low moan that followed, like a chorus from asthmatic organ pipes, confirmed what his nose was telling him. The re-animates were here, and they were hungry.

Lillian caught her breath as she saw them. At this distance, there was no way she could see detail. Which was a blessing in disguise. Even if this lot had re-animated just before they left the nearest Project base, the journey in a closed container, the only safe way to transport re-animates, wouldn't have done them any favors. The heat and minor wounds caused by rattling around in the thing meant they were starting to degrade and, by the smell wafting up the corridors, they'd already started to snack on one of their number.

"That's them?" she whispered.

Jack didn't get time to answer. The groan increased, gaining in pitch and volume. The shuffling separated out into the patter of running feet.

"Incoming," he yelled, bringing his rifle into his shoulder. "Fire at will!"

All hell broke loose. The first RA into the line of fire had been a young man. A prisoner, by the looks of the jumpsuit. These days, lethal injection was the least of your worries if you were stupid enough to end up on death row. Thanks to a governmental mandate, if you were sentenced to death your ass belonged to science. Or, more specifically, the Project. Just more grist for the RA mill.

His eyes were fixed on where Darce, Sanders and Nic stood. Drool dripped from his chin and he moaned hungrily, lurching toward them with a single-minded intensity common in re-animates. Once they got an idea fixed in their decaying heads, that was it.

He didn't make two steps before the air was alive with bullets. They slammed into him, his dead body jumping and jerking like a marionette on speed. The projectiles tore through his clothing, shredding flesh, muscle and bone as though it were paper. They didn't leave wounds, just ragged holes that leaked corrupt blood.

Jack didn't stop firing, even when the first RA was joined by others in an overwhelming press. He targeted limb joints. Knees, ankles, hips. If the things couldn't run, they were easier to put down.

"Thomas," he yelled over the din. "RAs down, shotgun. Darce, get your fur on. We got runners."

Chapter Eleven

If Lillian thought her life had turned into a horror movie before, then the reality of seeing real "live" zombies up close and personal rocked her to the core. Her eyes widened as the first one came into view. She'd dealt with patients from all walks of life and in all stages of mental illness. The shuffling gait and empty eyes were things she saw with highly medicated cases. But there was something else, something so inherently wrong about the man in front of her, that her brain instantly rejected the evidence of her eyes.

He was walking and talking...if you could call the sound he was making speech...but he was dead. Totally and utterly dead, his eyes were devoid of life and starting to whiten.

"Holy s—"

The rest of her sentence was cut off as the soldiers around her opened fire. She'd never been in a firefight, only ever seen them in the movies. The real thing was *nothing* like it was onscreen.

It was a loud, chaotic maelstrom of noises and smells. The thunder of weapons firing, spent casings hitting the floor combined with the smell of cordite and burnt, rotting flesh. It overwhelmed her senses as she cowered behind Jack, dropping her axe to the floor as she clapped her hands over her ears and hated herself for her weakness. She couldn't see or hear anything.

She'd wanted a gun? Ha! What a joke. She'd have dropped it in shock as soon as the shit hit the fan.

Pulling her trusty fire axe closer with a foot, she bit her lip and tried not to whimper as she waited for the firing to stop. A shadow cast by the moonlight outside flitted across the floor in front of her. She frowned. There was only her, Jack and his team in the corridor, and they were all concentrating on killing zombies.

It had to have come from outside, perhaps a cloud covering the moon. She looked up, and her heart almost stopped. There were more zombies outside. Her heart pounding in her chest, she clambered to her feet, back against the wall and axe in hand.

This part of the corridor was outside the secure area. Which meant that the gates at the end Jack and his men were firing through were the start of the secure zone. It also meant that the French windows at the end of this corridor, just out of sight around the corner, weren't barred.

"Shit."

She edged a couple of steps down the corridor, trying to crane her neck enough to see around the corner without having to get too close to it. There was no way she'd hear glass breaking, not with the chaos behind her. Were the zombies intelligent enough to break the glass to gain entry, or would they mill about looking for an open door? The doors wouldn't be open. They might not be barred, but they would be locked and bolted.

The sounds behind her changed. The gunfire died down, replaced by shotgun blasts, snarls and growls. The sickening sound of tearing flesh reached her ears. Refusing to check behind her, she padded down the hall, one hesitant step at a time, with her axe raised high.

She jumped as another shadow flitted past her. Shit, surely that was too fast for one of the zombies? Her heart pounded a frantic tattoo against her ribcage. Taking a deep breath to calm herself, she ventured another couple of steps closer. Even at a run, that first zombie hadn't been that quick. The movement she'd seen had to have been an owl or something that time. There were a couple who lived in the trees on the edge of the hospital grounds.

Fortifying herself with logic, she edged to the corner. Her arms ached, but she kept the axe high, just in case. Movement fluttered in the corner of her eye. She screamed and swung the axe wildly.

The blade slammed into the wooden frame of the window, burying itself deep. The sharp blade had sheared the fluttering net curtain nearly in two, the bottom half falling away to hang like a dejected flag.

"Fucking piece of shit," she muttered as she tried to yank it free. Some Xena-type she'd made. Losing it as the first twitch of a curtain. Hopefully no one had noticed…

"Okay, who let the civilian have the axe?"

Color burned across her cheeks as the comment dropped right into a lull in the snarling and fighting. *Typical, just typical.* She'd fucked up, and the eyes of the world were on her. Swearing at the axe, she tried everything but putting her foot on the frame to jerk it loose. Knowing her luck, if she tried that, her foot would slip and she'd end up on her backside with her legs in the air.

"Leave it, Lillian. We have more than enough weaponry." Jack spared her a look over his shoulder as he reloaded. Beyond him, the formerly pristine corridor resembled a massacre. Moans, groans and things moving in the bloody mess made her turn away quickly.

She heaved on the axe again. She wasn't leaving it. It was *her* axe. The world had gone to hell in a hand basket, so if she wanted to carry it around like some lethal, sharp edged security blanket she damn well would.

The hairs rising on the back of her neck warned her that something was amiss. Her gaze latched onto the tiny flutter in the severed curtain. The windows should be closed for the night. Where had the breeze come from?

She froze, her gaze sliding sideways as she tried to look behind her without moving her head. Terror welled up in the center of her chest and threatened to overflow. A shuffle. A whimper of fear escaped her lips. There was someone...no, some*thing...*behind her.

As if it could read her thoughts, the thing behind her moaned. A sound of animal, mindless hunger it grabbed the terror running rampant through her body, added a little imagination and took it on a joyride. Images of the things surrounding her and stripping the flesh from her body filled her mind.

Visions of teeth and claw-like fingers digging deep into her unprotected belly to pull forth blood-covered gobbets of flesh tormented her. Her body stiffened in terror and her bowels fluttered, a precursor to loss of control.

"Like *fuck*!"

Grabbing the axe, she wrenched it from the doorframe in one almost super-human wrench. Swinging it over her head like some modern-day female Conan the Barbarian, she slammed it into the neck of the zombie standing right behind her. The force of the blow separated its head from its neck, thick black fluid splattering up the wall beside her. The body sighed as the remaining gas escaped dead lungs and collapsed in a messy sprawl on the ground.

"These are new pants, asshole. I'm not pissing them for *anyone!*"

The RAs in the corridor were dealt with. Mostly. The three part-turned wolves moved between the groaning corpses, decapitating those who still had heads. Most didn't. Standard operating procedure with re-animates was to take out the leg joints, then pop the head with as much ammo as it took or a close-quarter shotgun blast. It wasn't pretty and left bits of skull on your clothes, but it was the most effective way to kill the bastards. If you were out of ammo, then you had to get up close and personal with your claws, something none of the team liked to do. It took weeks to get the stink off your skin.

Now he finally had time to draw breath, Jack looked around for Lillian, expecting to see her still struggling with the axe in the window frame. A smile curved his lips. He'd tease her about that later. His fierce little warrior woman.

The scene that met his eyes all but stopped his heart right in his chest. A re-animate stood right behind Lillian, its hand reaching out to grab her hair...

"Noooooooooo!"

He was on his feet, and propelling himself toward her without conscious thought. His beast roared at the threat to the woman it had decided was theirs.

"*Stand to*!" He heard but ignored the shout behind him. "RAs at the rear!"

The change ripped through him in a quarter of a second, his body distorting and changing in the space between one footstep and the rest. His clawed feet, still human in shape, dug gouges in the floor.

Ten feet. He wasn't going to reach her in time. She was going to die and all because he wouldn't give her a gun. A roar of frustration and fury erupted from his massive chest.

Five feet. She tightened her grip on the stuck axe, her knuckles white with the strain and ripped it from the wood. As he watched, she swung the thing like a pro.

He hit the corner as the head rolled across the floor. Just in time. Another RA rounded the turn at a run, its dead eyes fixed on Lillian. He slid the last few yards, his claws squealing against the floor. Dropping to a crouch in front of his woman, Jack snarled, the sound low and deadly.

The dead creature in front of him, a woman this time, just chittered hungrily. Her jaw worked as she stared at Lillian, as though she was already chewing on fresh meat, drool dripping from her chin to stain her blouse. She'd been dead a while, her skin green and her abdomen distended. Almost at the end of her usable life for the Project—any more decay and she would no longer be viable as anything other than fertilizer. For some reason the women always decayed faster than the men.

The snarl spilling from his throat grew louder and became a growl. In the corner of his eye, he saw one of the guys, Palmer, retrieve Lillian from behind him. Good, he didn't want her in the line of fire when he ripped this thing up. Just one slash of bodily fluids into any small cut she had and she'd be infected. If that happened, he'd put a bullet through her brain himself.

They said the RAs didn't retain their memories, that there was just hunger and the instinct to kill. Even so, it was a horror he was not going to subject her to. Not while he had breath in his body.

The re-animate stepped to the side and tried to skirt around him to follow Lillian. Jack batted it back with a casual swipe of his claws. Dead flesh parted under the razor-sharp talons. The smell of putrefaction blossomed on the air. He wrinkled his nose in disgust.

Jeez, these things needed a bath. Or a bonfire. Oh crap. He would not think of barbecue. He would not think of barbecue.

Luckily for him, he didn't get time. Seeing its next meal disappearing around the corner, the thing howled in frustration and rushed him. Jack met it at a run, his heavy thighs powering him forward. They collided in the middle of the corridor, and he wrapped huge, distorted hands around the thing's ribcage. His talons slid into the rotten skin with a small *snick* he felt more than heard. Without a flicker of pain, it snarled and snapped at him with blunt teeth.

He snarled right back, his lips curling from his muzzle and revealing all the wickedly sharp teeth within. With a heave of his inhumanly broad shoulders, he snapped the ribcage like kindling, tossing the broken halves against opposite walls. Decapitation may have been the approved method of dispatching a re-animate, but not having a body for the head to sit on worked just as well.

She couldn't stop shaking.

Lillian sat curled in a little ball tucked between the wall and a heavy steel cabinet and concentrated on stopping the tremors raking her body. She tried, honest to goodness tried, but it appeared to be Mission Impossible.

"I did it," she told the kind-faced soldier who knelt down in front of her. He'd been the one who'd pulled her away when the wolfman—Jack—had come crashing to her rescue.

She hadn't even *seen* the second zombie. Before she could do anything about it, even with her trusty axe, Jack had been there, and Palmer had herded her back down the corridor. He'd even taken her axe from her, something they'd had a minor tussle over. In the end though, no matter how much of an ass-kicking, zombie-killing bitch she was, she couldn't hold out against werewolf strength and he'd won.

"I know, you did good," he said with a smile. It wasn't a patronizing smile, like the ones she'd seen earlier. His eyes sparkled with genuine pleasure.

"Perfect swing, you took the thing's head off clean at the shoulder. Do you know how hard it is to do that? We should call you Killer."

Unable to help herself, she matched his grin with one of her own. Even though she was horrified at what she'd done, taken the life of a "living" thing, she knew without a shadow of a doubt she'd do it again if she had to.

Click click click. The noise of claws against linoleum filled the corridor and Lillian paused. She'd had pet dogs as a kid, so she knew the sound of paws when she heard it. And these sounded like some seriously large paws.

Looking up, her gaze collided with Palmer's. He reached down and picked up her hand. His eyes were human-green at the moment, but she knew that the same sort of creature that dwelled within Jack lived in him too.

"Deep breath," he advised, with a wry twist of his lips. "We can't have Killer freaking out, now can we?"

The words startled a laugh out of her as she looked around. The same concerned expression as in Palmer's eyes looked back at her from the rest of them. They were all worried about her freaking out. Like, seriously worried about it. The concern from people she'd only known for hours touched her heart.

She patted Palmer's hand. "I just decapitated an extra from *The Walking Dead.* With an axe. I think I can handle a little doggy, don't you?"

There was what sounded suspiciously like a snort from behind Palmer, but the soldier ignored it. A twinkle of amusement in his eyes, he inclined his head.

"Okay. If you're sure."

He stood up, still holding her hands so she was forced to stand with him. It was that or be dragged. Despite her brave words, she was glad for the support. Apprehension didn't just hum through her body, it was using her network of veins as a racetrack, urged on by the frantic beat of her heart.

She knew what she was going to see as Palmer pulled her away from the wall. Focusing her eyes on the edge of the cabinet, she watched as her view of the corridor rotated. The expanse of wall panned to the left and the window came into view. The net curtain hung lifeless, like a sail on a windless sea.

Comforted by that, she looked along the floor. A pair of clawed paws came into view first. Her breath caught. They were huge, ending in vicious claws designed for slicing and rending, covered in the black blood she was coming to associate with the zombies.

She followed the paws upward into legs and farther on into broad shoulders. A muzzle dropped down into view, and she found herself face to face with the biggest wolf she'd ever seen in her life. He'd changed from the weird half-man, half-wolf thing that had attacked the zombie into a creature any human would recognize.

Fear exploded and held her captive. Her natural instincts screamed at her to run, to escape. Although her conscious mind told her that this wasn't a wolf, that it was Jack, her survival instincts knew a predator when it saw one. Instincts that had shaped the human race's evolution over millennia and were hard as hell to suppress.

But suppress them she did, keeping her gaze locked onto

the creature in front of her. He didn't move, just looked back at her as her mind argued with itself. This was Jack. Just at the thought of him, the image of his face presented itself in her mind. A sense of safety and security accompanied it. Biting her lip, she tried to reconcile that with the massive beast in front of her. She trusted Jack, and this *was* Jack. Just another version of him.

Oh, don't be so damn stupid! You've seen zombies ready to snack on your brains. He's a werewolf, for heaven's sake. Probably buttering you up for dinner later!

She squashed the nasty little voice, shoving it into the smallest box in the back of her mind. Disengaging her hands from Palmer's, she took a step toward Jack. Her eyes were everywhere, from the claws to the tufted ears to the broad expanse of his back. Hell, he was so big he could double as a pony for a small child.

Could she trust him? She'd only met him yesterday and it had been a whirlwind ride ever since. As soon as she thought it, her gaze collided with his and she had her answer.

Warm amber radiated concern and worry in a mirror image of the expressions his men had worn. Concern for her, and worry...worry about what? He shuffled his feet, dropped his head a little. At the despondent line of his shoulders and the little whuffle he gave, it hit her. He was worried about what she thought. Of him.

"You silly thing," she breathed and rushed him. She closed the gap between them within a heartbeat. Wrapping her arms around his neck, she buried her face in the heavy fur. It was softer than she'd imagined, like silk against her skin.

"You're beautiful. Absolutely beautiful."

Chapter Twelve

Silence filled the corridor as she stood with her face buried in the thick fur at Jack's neck. His fur was soft and fluffy underneath, with coarse hair on top, and smelled of pure Jack. Closing her eyes, she burrowed her fingers under the coarse hair to the soft and just rested against him. The rest of the world fell away for a few precious seconds. She knew when she opened her eyes it would all still be there. The blood-splattered corridor, the destroyed corpses and the silent, not-human soldiers. She didn't care. Just for a moment she wanted to block it all out and pretend she was safe.

Claws clicked on the floor behind her. Lots of claws. Jack whuffed softly and moved under her hold. She lifted her head and turned, peeking out from behind Jack's scarred ear. Three more wolves walked up the corridor, padding through what remained of the zombie bodies. Paws black with zombie blood, two were easily as big as Jack was, but the third was smaller. With white fur and ice-blue eyes, she was easy to identify.

"Nic?"

The white wolf dipped her head as though nodding and looked up at Lillian through thick lashes. The anger Lillian had sensed in her in human form was still there but muted, as though she were happier as a wolf.

The wolf on the left was the leaner of the other two, and

much smaller than Jack. His dark-gold eyes weren't familiar, but the sandy-blond fur and the way he hunched his shoulders tipped her off.

"Sanders." It had to be, and he was just as quiet as a wolf as he was as a man.

Shifting from foot to foot, she looked at the last wolf and met warm amber eyes that sparkled with mischief. She grinned in reply. "And you have to be Darce."

"Keep this up and you'll spark some new urban legends. The Lycan Whisperer. You'll be famous!" Palmer chuckled. At her look, he shrugged. "Not even the doctors back at base can work out who's who when we've shifted. Well, apart from Nic and the boss-man. Our gal's coloring is too distinctive to be missed, and the captain's too big. The rest of us are too similar in wolf form."

She lifted an eyebrow, surprised at that, and looked back at Sanders and Darce. "But it's easy to spot who's who. It's in their eyes, the way they hold themselves."

Before Palmer could add more, the sound of running feet echoed down the corridor. Richards, sent to spy on the troops outside, skidded around the corner, hopped neatly over the pile of bodies and came to stop between the hulking forms of Sanders and Darce, followed at a run by the remaining two members of the squad, who'd introduced themselves earlier as Blake and Thom. She wondered what their wolves would look like, what aspect of their human appearance or mannerisms would cross over to their lupine forms.

"Move your big ass, LT," Thom quipped as he almost collided with Darce, and the trio looked at Jack.

"Still got the commandos out there, and that female Blood. Choppers show no sign of giving it up either..." Richards stopped and looked around the small group. "We're trapped."

She froze, picking up her cue from the silent men and wolves around her. Trapped wasn't good. They'd already sent zombies in, so what were they going to send next? Dracula? They'd already said there was a vampire out there, so...Bride of Dracula?

Jack dropped his head and slid out from under her arm. Feeling an immediate sense of loss, she tried not to pout and stepped away as he started to change. Like before, it was like a scene out of a cheap horror movie as his fur receded, swallowed up into his skin as bones popped and skin stretched. Unlike with Darce in the cell, this was quick. Under the influence of silver, Darce had seemed unsure about what shape he needed to be, but Jack certainly knew. Within seconds, he'd shifted forms, and a familiar figure crouched where the big wolf had been.

A familiar and very naked figure.

Oh my. Her eyes widened as he uncurled himself and stood. She knew the ripped physique, the toned muscles. She was even visually acquainted with his tight-as-hell ass. The light smattering of hair that followed the center line of his toned abs, teasing her earlier by disappearing into his pants, was fully revealed now. It arrowed down his flat stomach and beyond to thin out just before it reached his groin. Her eyes widened as she got a glimpse of his cock, but before she could blush, or even look away, Palmer moved and a bundle of cloth hit Jack in the middle of the chest.

"For fucks sake, put it away, boss man. Some of us don't want your one-eyed staring us in the face."

A grin twisted the Alpha's lips as he started to pull the pants on. "Button it. We all know you're just jealous." The banter slid from his lips without apparent thought because the next moment Jack's expression was serious.

"Now, listen up," he said, his voice calm and collected. "Because I'm going to make this short and sweet."

The squad moved closer, even the wolves. Lillian found herself between the furry bulk of Darce and the smooth-skinned heat of Jack's half-naked body. The absurdity of the situation hit her as as he started to talk. She was stuck between a wolf and a guy who looked like he'd stepped out of a Hollywood blockbuster. Oh yeah, and they were about to battle zombies and could die. It sucked to be her.

"We're trapped like rats in a cage, and the enemy is knocking on the door. They sure as fuck ain't here to borrow a cup of sugar. Oh no, they're breathing down our necks with a Blood, flamethrowers..."

The three wolves pulled their lips back and snarled at the word. She guessed that even though they were human some of the time, the instinctive fear of fire was still strong.

"And a couple of gunships. You know why? Because we're different. They made us what we are, but they can't control us. They opened Pandora's box, and now they're shitting themselves because they can't close it. So they made themselves judge, jury and executioner...and our numbers are up."

Jack paused for breath as he finished buttoning his pants. "But you know what? Fuck 'em." His snarl echoed along the tiled walls of the corridor. "They might be Project, they might be human—most of them—but they are now the enemy, and they should be in no doubt we are their nemesis."

Her breath caught at the power and conviction in his voice. It sounded very much like one of those "we're outnumbered, behind enemy lines, let's take as many of the enemy with us" speeches from just about any of the war movies she'd seen.

"I know I'm not going to make it. But this has been coming

since they shoved that virus in my veins and made me into what I am. But that's cool. I just didn't make it out this time."

"Hmmm, Jack?" she tried to interrupt, but her soft query fell on deaf ears, buried under his impassioned speech.

"But the line must be drawn. Here." He pointed savagely at the ground. "Here and no further. Here they learn what pissing off a Lycan pack means. If we're damned, then let's be damned for what we *really* are."

"Jack," she tried again, her voice louder this time. "You don't need to. I think I have—"

He wasn't listening to her, too caught up in the drama of the moment.

"We've got to get mad to fulfill that promise, to fuel the fire and prove to them that they do *not* want to fuck with us. That they can start the fight, but we *will* finish it."

"Jack, there's a way out."

"This is our time…this is *our* day. This is—"

"Would you *shut up and listen, you stupid mutt?"*

The silence after her shout was so complete that the sound of a pin dropping would have deafened. All eyes swiveled toward Lillian, the stunned expression on their faces so comical that, if the situation hadn't been so bad, she'd have burst out laughing.

Nic slid to the floor and covered her nose with her paws. Beside her, Darce's gold-amber eyes sparkled with amusement. Jack was the first to find his voice.

"Did you just call me a mutt?" he asked carefully.

"Yes! Fur, paws…" she gestured vaguely in his direction. "Selective deafness. Just like my aunt's lab. He always ignores me unless I have food for him. So…mutt."

A sense of amusement rippled through the pack, Palmer putting voice to it. "A lab. Yeah, I can see that… Boss does look kinda lab-like. It's around the ears, I think."

If looks could kill, Palmer would have keeled over from the furious glare Jack shot him.

"Well, darling, you have all my attention now. What's so important you have to call me a mutt?"

"Don't forget the lab part." Richards grinned.

Jack ignored the muttered comment in favor of looking at her. His eyes were solid amber. She sucked a breath in, not in fear, not entirely. There was something almost hypnotic about him. She knew he wouldn't hurt her, not really, but the element of danger thrilled her right down to her toes.

"Oh, yes!" Fighting the pull of his unusual eyes she forced herself to remember what she'd been going to say. "There's a way out. There's an old maintenance tunnel, leads to the old boiler house. It's gone now, the boiler house, but the tunnel's still there."

"And you're sure this isn't on the modern plans?"

Jack still couldn't believe his luck as, back in their impromptu war room, Lillian spread an old map over the architect's plans they'd been looking at earlier. Part of him wanted to howl in frustration. If she'd just told him about this earlier, they could've gone before the RAs got here.

"Nope, not at all."

She shook her head as she finished spreading the map out and leaned over it. Her ample breasts pressed against the thin blouse she wore. His gaze riveted to the delectable sight. The swell of the luscious globes winked at him, peaking above the deep vee of her neckline. His mouth watered, his body reacting in an instant.

Jack ignored the reaction and forced himself to concentrate on the map in front of him. It was old, the paper beginning to yellow, and hand-drawn in the style of a bygone era. He traced the lines with his finger. There was a whole level missing from the new plans.

"The architect who came to survey the place was a sleaze...more interested in hitting on the female staff and making cracks about funny farms. Since he was only interested in the other wing, I figured he didn't need to know about the sub-basement level in this one. Besides, I'd have been tempted to lock him down there and throw away the key," she admitted with a wry grin.

He followed a narrow set of lines, which cut off with a wavy symbol. "The tunnel?"

She nodded. "Yeah. It re-appears here, coming up under the old boiler house. The structure's gone now, there's a little copse out in the gardens to provide visual interest for the patients instead. The tunnel itself should be sound, though. I checked it out about six months back, and there were no signs of damage or imminent collapse. I think... I'm no expert, though."

A combined mixture of relief and admiration, he allowed the grin that had been lurking to emerge and spread across his lips. They had a way out. He could get his men, and Lillian, to safety. Heat filled his body as he slid a caressing glance over her curvy figure again. When they were somewhere safe, he was going to take her to bed. Claim her, mark her, make her his and his alone.

Chapter Thirteen

"Shhh, sound carries well through the ventilation ducts," Lillian scolded as the wolf pack crowded past her, chattering between themselves as they congregated on the small landing. Below them, the stairs reached down into the darkness. Not one of them seemed willing to move off the top step without their petite, human guide. Jack's lips quirked. Big, scary werewolves, afraid of the dark.

"Unless you want our friends up there figuring out there's another way out of here, I suggest you all keep it shut."

She pulled the door closed, slender muscles standing out under her delicate skin. A pang of guilt hit Jack; he hadn't realized how heavy the thing was. At least three wolves, himself included, started to step forward to help, but she'd already managed it. The door hit the frame with a resonant clang.

"Shit."

Everyone in the small corridor froze. Jack expanded all his senses. Around him, he could hear the thunder of Lillian's heart, a rapid counter-point to the slower, deeper beats of the wolf pack; the sound of water rushing through the pipes that ran under their feet; and somewhere overhead, the metallic tick-tock of an old-style clock.

Nothing happened. No shouts. No thunder of running feet. After a few long moments, he released the breath he'd been holding.

"I think we're good. They must be too far away to have heard it. And human hearing is crap anyway...no offense."

Lillian shrugged. "None taken. At least I don't smell like wet dog."

On cue, the wolves around her all started to sniff their armpits, trying to hide what they were doing with coughs or running their hands through their hair. Apart from Nic, who just glared at the shorter woman. Jack grinned as she caught his gaze, her eyes alight with amusement. He didn't know how she'd done it, but she'd figured out his pack quicker than he had. From scolding them to teasing insults, she was spot on.

"She's just messing with you. Quit screwing around and get moving. After you, my lady."

Primly, she stepped past him. Pausing at the top of the stairs, she looked at the heavy, baton-like flashlight in her hand. A flick of her thumb on the switch later, the stairwell was bathed in strong, white light.

"Arrrrgggghh!" Darce warbled. "Bright light. Bright light!"

Jack sighed. There was always one.

"Ignore him," he advised when Lillian looked back in concern. Reaching out, he swatted his second in command around the back of the head. "He's an ass."

"Ahhh, okay." She started down the steps, the flashlight highlighting the steps in front of her. "Watch how you go down here, some of the steps are wet."

Lillian led them down the steps and into a short tunnel-like corridor. Although it only had one door, the tunnel continued into a dead end. At Jack's curious look, she shrugged again.

"There were some notes on the old plans about extending

this section, but then the original owner died. His son decided not to continue with the development."

She paused with her hand on the door in front of her and looked over her shoulder. "He's the one mainly responsible for all the things we keep down here. Equipment," she clarified as a couple of the wolves frowned. "From the darkest times of the hospital's history."

She pushed open the door and ushered them inside. Jack was last through the door, making sure that no one could creep up on them from behind. Lillian might have locked the door, but they had a Blood up there and Jack didn't trust those things as far as he could throw them. Bloods and Lycans, born from the same research but enemies as soon as they'd come into existence.

As soon as he stepped through into the storage room, he stopped, eyes wide and all senses open as he looked around. It was full of medical-type junk, leaving only a few walkways through the clutter. Lillian pulled the door to behind them and panned the flashlight around. Shackles hung next to straightjackets on the wall, near a bathtub with a barred lid that left only a gap for someone's neck.

"Ice-bath therapy. Non-consensual."

Lillian's voice was quiet and composed as she explained each item the light fell upon. "Restraint chairs...restraint box. Patients were locked into these things for hours. You can still see the scratches they left on the arms of the chairs."

She moved farther into the room, the wolves spanning out around her, unable to resist having a poke around. Jack paused by one of the chairs to look at the gouges in the wood of the arms. A dark stain farther down caught his attention. He knelt and ran his hand over it. The scent of old blood rose like a fetid cloud. He coughed to clear his lungs and stood. Someone had died in that chair, beaten until their blood ran down the legs and stained the wood.

He shuddered. And the project called him and his men animals.

“What are these? They look like ice picks.”

He turned to find Darce holding up a small metal pole that did indeed look very much like an icepick. In fact, it looked so much like one that he flicked a glance at the stuff around Darce, expecting to see some snowshoes or crampons.

Lillian moved to his side to look. Unlike the wolves, she didn’t have enhanced night vision. With the residual light from the flashlight, the room was lit up like daylight for Jack and his men.

“Ah, yes. That’s a nasty little surgical tool. It’s an orbitoclast.”

Darce looked puzzled, turning it over in his hand and testing the point. “Surgical? It’s not even sharp.”

“Doesn’t need to be. It’s for performing lobotomies.”

Nic, over the other side of the room, chuckled. “Well, Darce’ll be safe then. His brain’s in his d—”

“Bite me.” Darce cut her off, shooting a glare across the room hot enough to flay even wolf flesh from bones. Jack sighed. Great, the female wolf was even getting to the normally levelheaded lieutenant.

“Nah, you’d enjoy it too much. You and your fan—”

“*Enough*!” Jack’s snarl cut across the forming argument. “In case you two hadn’t noticed, this isn’t a walk around the local museum with tea and fucking cookies afterwards. Now get your shit together and let’s move out.”

Neither wolf would look at him, turning their faces away as he walked between them. As he expected. Neither were ready, or wanted, to challenge his authority as Alpha. That was a decision that would land them in a world of hurt and they both knew it.

"What *is* up with you?" he turned to hiss at Darce. "Nic I can understand. She's been on the edge since she was turned, but you? You've got more freaking sense."

Before Darce could answer him, there was a low snarl from behind him. Jack turned, expecting to see her squaring up to Darce, only to find Nic backing up with sheer terror on her face. She tripped and fell on her ass but carried on backpedaling, her feet scrabbling on the slick flagstones. A low-level keen of distress escaped her throat.

"Shit!" If there was anything he recognized instantly, it was a wolf about to lose it. "Sanders, grab her."

Jack moved like lightening, sliding his bigger body between Nic and whatever had set her off. In the same instant, Sanders hauled her to her feet, easily wrapping the woman in his arms.

Cool, calm and collected, Sanders had always been able to deal with the volatile female. Jack suspected it was because the guy preferred men. There was no question of him being interested in her on a male-female level.

She turned and buried her face against his neck, her shoulders shaking. She was crying. Nic, the queen-bitch of the pack, was crying. Eyes wide, Jack turned to find out what had made her crack.

At the sight of the wooden box, he drew a sharp breath. Instinctively his wolf snarled within, yammering to get away. To run from the foul thing before he could be caught and forced back inside it. The size of a coffin, its sides were made of bars, and the base a thin mattress over yet more bars. Cramped, there was enough room for an adult human to lie down but not turn over when the lid was closed and locked.

That was the point. It was designed to hold its victim immobile and helpless for however long deemed necessary. The Project used them when they made his kind. A newer version, not like this wooden one, but one made of silver and steel. They locked their "subjects" within the things, and with just one drop of LY16…that was all it took.

Jack closed his eyes as memory threatened to overwhelm him. A room with row after row of metal cages…fighting both the drugs and the guards as they fought to trap him in one…flat on his back, looking through the bars as the needle came closer…the power and pain as the virus raced through his body…screams of agony as the injection forced some of the subjects to change right there, the metal bars not giving as their suddenly larger forms were crushed within.

A growl rumbled up from his soul, finding voice through the medium of his chest and throat.

"No. We are not slaves to fear."

Opening his eyes, he looked at the hated object again. "It's a box, just a box. Nothing that can hold us. Nothing can ever hold us anymore."

"This is the way out. I'm sorry, I should have warned you about that… I didn't think."

Lillian's voice was a welcome balm as she unlocked the last door and opened it. The scent of earth and rain filled the small room, the smell of the forest and freedom carried to them on a gentle breeze.

"No, it's not your fault. You had no way of knowing."

Shaking his head, Jack watched as Sanders, flanked by the other members of the pack, half-carried the shaking female through the door and into the darkness beyond.

"There's only one tunnel, with steps at the end," Lillian explained, her lovely eyes filled with concern for the other woman. “Will she be okay?”

“Yeah, once she scents freedom, she’ll shift and run. Fight or flight syndrome. She’s all front. Really, she’s the most fragile of all of us. Mentally, that is. Apart from this idiot.”

Jack nodded as Darce joined them, still twirling the orbitoclast in his fingers. The rest of the wolves had followed Sanders and Nic to secure the other end of the tunnel.

“He’s just impressed he can lick his own balls now.”

Darce grinned. “Fucking too right. Every cloud’s got a silver lining!”

The sound of someone banging on the door at the top of the stairs froze the three of them in their tracks. Lillian gasped, her eyes wide in the light cast by the flashlight and her knuckles wide around it.

“Hey, there are tracks down here. Someone’s opened this door.” The voice was faint but audible. Suddenly, gunfire sounded.

“Shit, he’s shooting the lock out.” Adrenalin hit Darce’s system at Mach 1, pumping him full of energy and waking the rarely slumbering beast inside. Before either could argue, he bundled Lillian into Jack’s arms and pushed them both toward the tunnel door.

“Get her out of here, I’ll deal with this.”

“You sure, man?”

Jacks eyes mirrored his dilemma. The need to protect the tiny woman in his arms warred with his duty. The fact he didn’t like leaving one of his men behind was obvious, but Darce knew that anyway.

Whenever they went on operational, the captain was always the first in and the last out. He took the kind of damage most of them could only dream of, and still came out kicking ass. Darce had no idea how he did it.

"Totally. Now get out of here before I kick your ass and take your woman."

Jack snorted, amusement flooding his features as he stepped back to allow Lillian to enter the tunnel ahead of him. "When you're big enough. Catch you on the flip side, man. Remember..." He tapped his temple. "Think human."

Darce grinned as Jack ducked into the tunnel and out of sight. The grin widened as he closed the door and the room plunged into darkness.

"*Fuck* thinking human."

Even with the light gone, Darce could see easily in the pitch black, yet more proof that he wasn't anything close to human anymore. He reached out to snag something he'd seen earlier, and headed for the door. Once there, he stopped stock-still and listened. Outside, booted feet clunked down the steps. He could tell the guy was trying to be stealthy. It made no difference. He could hear the human as clearly as if he had decided to tap-dance in size twenty clown shoes.

Yet another plus for the furry side.

Marshaling his breathing, he concentrated. The darkness around him filled with the soft sound of joints popping and flesh sliding. He wasn't quite as adept at part-changing as Jack, but he could manage to shift his hands into grotesque almost-paws.

Snick...snick...snick.

Ignoring the pain, Darce felt a sense of satisfaction as his claws descended one by one. He'd never get tired of his ability to shift forms. Some of the guys had taken a while to get used to it, fearing the pain that always accompanied it. Not him. Sure, it hurt like a bitch, but it was an addictive hurt, like getting an armful of tattoos. No...better.

"This is fucking shit. They can't have come down here."

The whisper came as the human soldier paused on the other side of the door. Darce flexed his fingers, feeling the claws on the ends and smiled. Just a few inches of metal separated him from his prey. His heart pounded with the thrill of the hunt, and his sense sharpened. He could hear the thunder of the soldier's heartbeat, the scent of nervous sweat and barely controlled fear.

Darce shook his head. Hadn't this guy ever seen a horror film? There were three rules. The girl always got it first, never say "I'll be right back" and never under *any* circumstances go anywhere on your own...even if it was just to take a piss.

The door creaked. Darce held his breath as the human edged his way into the room. It felt like watching something out of *Silence of the Lambs*. He edged his way in farther, the thin line of his scope stabbing into the darkness. The dark swallowed it gleefully and just gave him glimpses of the nightmarish equipment hidden within it.

"Fuck me, what is this? This place is a fucking museum."

Darce slid into place behind the door as the guy did a full circle, looking at all the weird and wonderful stuff the wolves had picked over. With a silent movement, he slid the bolt back into place, confident the human couldn't hear anything over the racket of his own heart. Darce remembered the days, locked into a confining human body, with dull human senses. Things were much better now.

As the light flitted ever closer, he lifted the mask he'd picked from the random piles around him, covering his mouth. The light reached his face, almost blinding him.

"Hello, Clarice."

The soldier screamed like a girl and pulled the trigger.

Darce yelped, dropped the mask and dove behind the metal bath in the corner. Bullets peppered the wall and floor until the magazine ran out.

"Fuck fuck fuck fuck fuck!"

As the guy reloaded, Darce was on his feet and moving through the darkness.

"Little pig, little pig, you shouldn't have come in."

The new magazine slammed home with a click. Bullets slammed into the wall where Darce had been a moment before. Christ, even in the dark this guy was good. He'd only expect a seriously experienced soldier to aim sight-unseen. A soldier like him.

"*Screw you!*" the human screamed. It was an impressive show of rage, if not for the scent of terror staging an all-out assault on Darce's sensitive sense of smell. "I'll blow your head off, you mother-fucker."

"Not by the hair of my chinny-chin-chin."

He ducked and rolled again as another burst of gunfire lit up the basement. The straightjackets behind him got some extra ventilation. Could be handy, he mused as he scuttled silently to the other side of the room. Summer model, maybe.

Crouched in the darkness, he watched as his prey shone the scope wildly around the room, trying to location him. Fighting in enclosed spaces was always difficult. Without ear protection, any gunfire made your ears ring like fuck, but with them, you couldn't hear for shit anyway. Fighting in an enclosed space, in the dark, with an enemy who had excellent night-sight? Uh, yeah. He'd take a pass on that one, thank you very much.

"Where are you? Come out here and fight like a man, you fucking coward."

"That's kinda the point, isn't it? I'm *not* a man. I'm an animal. An animal you and your buddies came to put down."

Darce kept moving as the human took pot shots into the darkness. As he moved into the center, the strange shape of the basement walls echoed the sound of his voice and made it impossible to tell where he actually was.

"How much ammo do you have?" He squinted a little and read the tape on the front of the uniform. Reaching out, he picked up a random manacle. "How long before you're left down here in the dark unarmed, Kelwood?"

As he spoke, he threw the cuff. It landed behind Kelwood, making him jump and spin around. The scope light shuttered, blinking as its power drained. Darce shook his head. *Rookie mistake. Always check the batteries.*

Padding up behind Kelwood, he stopped less than a foot away and waited. He knew the instant the human sensed his presence. He stiffened and turned his head slightly. Darce knew without a doubt that he wished he could see through the back of his own skull.

He leaned forward, level with the guy's ear.

"Boo."

The word was a soft pop, but the guy jumped like Darce had yelled at the top of his lungs. He turned, lifted the rifle at the same time as he pulled the trigger. Darce knocked it from his hands. The rifle hit the deck and skittered out of reach, its scope light flickering over the glistening floor.

Kelwood bellowed and went after it, but Darce moved too quickly. Lunging forward he batted the guy's trailing heel and took him off balance. He hit the deck with over two hundred pounds of lean, mean werewolf wrapped around him.

The scuffle on the floor was short and sweet. Even if Darce didn't outweigh and outreach him, Kelwood was human and he wasn't. Easily, he pinned the human down, a massive clawed paw around his throat, and leaned in so Kelwood could see him in the little light available.

"I'll huff, and I'll puff, and I'll tear your fucking th—"

He paused. This close to the guy, myriad new scents wafted up to him from the open neck of his combat uniform. Terror over-rode everything like an overweight back seat driver, but underneath there were other scents. Shower gel, the meatloaf he'd had a couple of nights ago, a woman's perfume perhaps rubbed off this morning when he'd kissed his significant other goodbye...and another scent. Warm, sweet and chillingly unmistakable.

"Fuck me. You got kids?"

Kelwood looked at him blankly, terror the sole expression on his face. "Huh?"

"Have. You. Got. Kids?"

That got his attention. The human's gaze latched onto his, barely flinching at the inhuman golden color. For a second, happiness filtered through the terror, and the werewolf knew Kelwood wasn't seeing him.

"Yeah. A little girl. She's four months old. Please...don't hurt them."

Darce shook his head and pulled back, hauling the smaller man to his feet. "And just how the fuck do you think I'm gonna manage that? In case it escaped your notice, we're in a basement in the middle of who-the-fuck-knows-where."

As he spoke, he walked across the basement, dragging the human in his wake.

"B-but, can't you read minds. Hypnotize us? You could've lifted my address from my head while talking to me." Kelwood moaned a noise of sheer panic. "Oh my God, you did, didn't you? Please don't hurt Alice, she's just a baby."

"Oh, for fuck's sake. We can't read minds or any other crap like that." Darce rolled his eyes, yanked open the lid of the wooden bed-cage, and stuffed the soldier into it. "And I've got better things to do that track down your family. Besides, babies scare the crap out of me."

He slammed the cage shut and bolted it. Looking back at Kelwood, he waited until the human looked him in the eye.

"I got a message for your boss. The Blood you got with you. Tell her that she's mine."

Chapter Fourteen

Whatever else Antonia had expected when she'd led her men into the shadowed hospital, it had not been to find a distinct lack of Lycans, remains or otherwise. Nor had she expected find the RAs torn limb from limb and spread over most of the corridor.

"Oh my God," Fletcher whispered. The squad stood in the middle of a massacre. Black blood pooled on the floor, extended up the walls.

"Fuck me...it's on the damn ceiling. How'd they get it up there?"

Antonia held her hand up for silence. Without a word, she studied the scene and breathed through her mouth so she could forget she even had a nose. The RAs smelled bad enough when they were in one piece. Broken up and tossed about like doggie chew toys...it turned even *her* stomach.

"They caught them in a cross-fire..."

They'd heard gunfire from outside but hadn't thought anything of it. The Lycans had been soldiers once upon a time. They knew the Project would send a clean-up team, so it stood to reason they'd arm themselves...presumably from the guards they'd killed.

It shouldn't have mattered. It was expected that they'd manage to take a few RAs out, but not all of them. Instinct would force them into a change, and any teamwork would disappear under feral instinct.

Her eyes narrowed as she counted the prints and tracks in the carnage. This was something else.

"Only three of them turned."

Surprise caught her blind-side as she walked through the battle scene. She paused in the middle of the blackened gore. A section of ribcage lay next to her foot, a line of intestine trailing toward what looked like half a pelvis. The rest of the body was lost in the chaos.

She didn't look too hard for it. At the moment the scene around her was abstract, like a set from a film, or a butcher's offal pile. If she looked too closely, her mind started to organize the mess, reminding her that these had once been people. People who had been slaughtered brutally.

Good thing they'd already been dead.

"Three turned, the others—"

She cut off her sentence right there. Something was wrong. Three of the Lycans had turned, and all research into the creatures said that once one shifted, the rest did as well. It was a chain reaction they couldn't control.

A frown creased her brow as she looked at the scene in front of her. The scientists had theorized that would be the next step in their evolution. First had been the ability to control their shifts, followed by the formation of loose packs. After that, they were supposed to mimic their counterparts in the wild and hunt together in animal form.

Fuck that. They *were* working as a team, but not on an animal level. Eyes wide, she spun around, putting the clues together. Once she knew what she was looking at, it was easy to see where the majority had cut down the RAs with automatic fire, leaving what was left to stumble into three fully shifted

Lycans who tore them apart limb from limb.

Admiration mingled with her instinctive hatred. How had they managed it? How had they kept their ability to work as a team secret under the very noses of the Project?

“Torch it.”

Stepping back she watched dispassionately as Fletcher and Perkins lit up. Within seconds, the corridor resembled a charnel house.

The two soldiers bathed the walls, floor and ceiling with gouts of flame, reducing blackened flesh and blood alike to a bubbling mass. Re-animate flesh burned easily and quickly, as though nature itself wanted to wipe it from existence. Acrid smoke rose from the remains, making the men behind Antonia gag and pull up their undershirts to cover their mouths and noses.

She stood unmoving.

The smell of the smoke didn’t bother her. It was sharp and foul, but it was cleansing. The purity of the fire burned the desecration away within minutes and left just the shattered bones to be collected.

The roar of the throwers stopped, and the two men looked around to see if there was anything they’d missed. It didn’t make much difference. They’d torch the entire wing before leaving anyway.

“Wilson, Fredericks…” she called out, already starting down the corridor her inhuman instincts told her was the way they’d gone. “Set the charges ready for us to leave, don’t set the timers. We got some mutts to find first.”

Leaving the two men to complete their assigned task, she motioned for the rest to follow her.

“Spread out, search the entire wing. There’s no way out so

they have to be in here somewhere. Work in twos and do *not* spilt up," she ordered, stopping by the doorway that had the highest concentration of Lycan scent.

"These things are stealth predators, so they'll try and pick you off one by one. Line of sight with your buddy at all times. You screw up, you've got me to deal with. Even if I have to RA your ass just so I can kick it from here to kingdom come. Move out."

The team scattered like the good little company men they were. Antonia managed to restrain the curl of her lip as she stepped through the door into the room she'd isolated.

Although her sense of smell wasn't as good as that of a Lycan, it was still sharper than it had been when she was human. She couldn't track a single trail with any accuracy, unless she'd taken blood from her prey, of course, but when the scents were piled one on top of each other, then even the most nasally challenged Blood could pick them up.

Standing by the door, she closed her eyes and breathed in. Lots of scents, all different. All with the heavy musky overtone she'd learned to expect from wolves. A minute passed, then another and still she stood there, learning the scents, separating them from one another. Eight...no, nine people. Her brow creased. They weren't all wolves. Hidden under the heavy musk was the clean, sharp copper scent of a human.

Her eyes snapped open, and she looked at the opposite wall blankly. Why did they have a human with them? Unless...no, it had to be a member of staff who'd been in the room just before the Lycans took it over. Strange, though, that there was no body. Perhaps they'd eaten it. It had been known before. A guard or scientist who let his guard down and ended up on the menu...

Animals.

She shook her head in disgust and prowled farther into the room, noting from the marks on the floor that the table had been dragged into the center. They'd crowded around it, further evidence of planning. What was on there? She moved closer and looked down at it. An architect's blueprint of the building looked back up at her.

"Clever little dogs."

There was something written on it. Putting a hand on the table to steady herself, she went to lean forward. As soon as her hand contacted the wood, heat and feral hunger slammed into her. An image of the Lycan she'd seen in the doorway earlier filled her mind.

Tall and heavily built, he had just the sort of warrior's physique she preferred in her men. Amber eyes were shadowed by the long, dark hair, but in her mind even the evidence of his other nature wasn't enough to put her off. In the privacy of her own head, she was free to ogle as much as she liked. Her mind was her own, much as it galled the Project to admit that.

As though her dream man could read her thoughts, he grinned, winked and blew her a kiss. The image faded from her mind as though it had never been.

"What the fuck?"

She tried to recall the image, but all she could bring to mind were her memories of earlier. The absurd thought that, somehow, Lycans were telepathic had her snatching her hand back from the table. Moving around it, she checked out the writing. It was nothing, just an architect's note added in pencil.

Crap. She sighed and closed her eyes tiredly. Today was going to hell in a handbasket, no mistake. Would it be too much to ask for a little break?

The sound of gunfire brought her head up sharply. Despite her instinct to race out of the door, she remained motionless for a second, her head tilted to one side as she isolated the direction the sound was coming from.

Down, she decided, and behind her. North.

She hit the door at a dizzying speed, even for a nonhuman, her hand clamped around the frame as she used it to spin her bodily into the corridor. The wood cracked sharply under her fingers. Ignoring it, she headed down the tile-lined hall. Perkins and his buddy emerged out of a room.

"Basement," she called out, past them before they could react and raise their rifles. If she'd wanted to kill them, they wouldn't have stood a chance. She was too quick for their dull human reactions. She just had to hope the Lycans hadn't developed the same kind of speed, because that would leave her facing a full pack on her own.

One Lycan she wouldn't mind. A particular Lycan with amber-gold eyes and dark hair... Heat and desire flushed through her cold body. The first carnal reaction—the first she'd had to a man, any man—since she'd been turned.

It was a surprising development. She'd assumed she'd died as a woman that day as surely as she'd died as a member of the human race. Locking it away in the bottom of her mind to consider later, she shoved the door to the basement open and charged down the steps, handgun in a firm grip.

The basement was empty. She raced through the adjoined rooms looking for the source of the gunfire. Someone had been down here. Several someones... No, several some*things*. She paused in the center of the last room and took a deep breath. Her guy had come this way. His scent wrapped around her like a lover's caress, making her lightheaded. Shaking her head to clear it she concentrated on the other scents, filtering through them one by one.

Her guy, the other Lycans and two human scents. One was

wrapped around the smell of cordite and camouflage cream. One of her team. The other was different, lighter and feminine but with an exotic twist that made her nose wrinkle. It was familiar, but she couldn't figure out where she'd smelled it before.

She dropped the thought in favor of following the scent trail. As she'd thought in the room upstairs, they *did* have a human with them. *But why? Hostage, entertainment...food?*

She edged into the last room, looking at it through her sights as she made sure it was clear. The one door in the opposite wall grabbed her attention. There wasn't supposed to be anything else down here. She had a photographic memory, another "gift" of her new nature. According to the plans upstairs, this was the last room. No door, no stairs beyond it.

A second later saw her with her back against the wall on one side of the door. Darkness coiled in the stairway beyond it. As soon as she stepped through it, the light of the basement behind her would put her in silhouette, the perfect target for someone waiting in the darkness beyond.

Her back against the rough plaster, clammy and wet from being so far beneath the earth, she opened her senses up and probed into the darkness. Unlike in popular myth and culture, the Project-created vampires had no spectacular supernatural abilities.

Sure, they were stronger and faster than humans, a *lot* stronger and faster than humans, and all their senses were enhanced. They could see better, hear better, their sense of smell was better. Turning into bats and leaping over fifty-foot buildings? Not so much. Although she had to admit, the ability to turn into a bat would be real useful right about now, if only for the echo-location. No, their abilities, when honed, were more in the mental spectrum.

She grinned at her own thought. Yeah, she was in a different mental arena all right.

There was no one waiting in the darkness of the stairwell. At least, if there was, they weren't breathing or making any other sound, even a heartbeat. Even the RAs, who had neither a heartbeat nor needed air, made some sort of sound. Usually, in their case, a low level groaning.

Confident in what her senses were telling her, Antonia stepped through the door and into the waiting darkness. Panic assaulted her for a split second as she was framed by the doorway. She'd been shot once, on her first operation as a rookie, because she'd been stupid enough to get caught in a doorway. The memory of bullets tearing into her flesh and the pain had never left her. It wasn't something she was particularly interested in trying again, even though these days bullets alone were unlikely to kill her.

Her boots were silent as she descended the stairs. There was a short corridor with only one door. The corridor though was longer than it needed to be, as though an extension had been intended but never gotten around to. *Interesting.*

Her breath plumed in the cold air. It had that sharp, damp quality about it that said they were deep in the bowels of the earth. A smile quirked her lips. Home sweet home for a vamp.

One door down here, one option. The sound of a heartbeat, as fast as a train racing on the tracks, reached her ears. Again the strange feminine scent of the woman with the wolves rose up to meet her, as though she'd paused here for longer than the others. As though she'd unlocked the door?

The knowledge expanded in her mind with such a sense of rightness she knew she couldn't be wrong. The woman was one of the staff. She had to be, there was no other explanation. Absorbing that fact, Antonia concentrated on the room beyond.

The scent was human, and the terrified mutterings told her it was one of her guys.

Hearing nothing else, she pushed the door open and strode into the room. The place was obviously used for junk storage. She stood for a second in the doorway, not needing any light to see. Relics that looked as if they belonged in a museum of horror packed the walls. She shivered. Humans scared themselves silly with stories of paranormal creatures and horror films, but the fact was they were the only monsters around.

"Oh, thank God. Please...please help me. I-I'm stuck."

The pathetic whimpering guided her through the maze of junk until she found the source. Locked into...*oh fuck*. Her eyes widened as she recognized the contraption Kelwood was pinned in. Basically a coffin with bars instead of sides, the Project was fond of using them for conversion. This was a wooden version. Even though it could be broken, by her at least, it still triggered all the same unpleasant associations.

She left him where he was. Stood over him with a grim expression on her face.

"Let me guess, you didn't play fetch?" she drawled, her arms folded. If he was stupid enough to get put in such a situation in the first place, then he deserved all he got.

He stopped struggling against the bars of the cage and just looked at her. His heart rate started to slow down, as though her presence was enough to calm him, and trust filled his eyes. Her lips quirked. *Welcome to the wonderful world of the Project, where dogs lock people in cages and vampires rescue them. Hollywood, eat your heart out.*

He muttered something as she leaned forward to undo the bolts on the top of the cage. Nothing as sophisticated as a lock for this baby. It had three crude but effective bolts holding the lid down and keeping the victim immobile. Once inside,

Kelwood couldn't even lift a hand to scratch his nose, so he hadn't a chance of reaching all three bolts to free himself.

"What did you say?"

She froze as she leaned over the cage and looked directly at him. Even though he knew what she was, he didn't flinch. She wanted to scream and rail at him not to trust her, not to trust anyone associated with the Project. She was just as inhuman as the Lycans who'd walked through here less than an hour ago, and just because she was on his side now didn't mean that would always be the case.

Kelwood's eyes flicked upward as she slid the bolt at the top back. "The guy in here, one of them...the Lycans. He gave me a message."

She paused on the last bolt and made a show of sniffing the air above the captured man. "A message. Did he scratch you?" Her voice was harsh, a little of her well-hidden temper leeching into her black on black eyes.

The human in the cage shivered. "No. He just said to tell you..."

The hesitance, although no doubt well-meaning, was really beginning to get on Antonia's nerves. Vampire 101, Bloods had neither a sense of humor nor any patience. At all.

"He said *what?*"

"He said..." The human swallowed and eyed her nervously, finally appearing to realize what a dangerous predicament he was in. "T-that you're his."

Chapter Fifteen

When he'd told her zombies were attacking, she'd asked for a gun. When he refused, she'd found an axe and armed herself. She'd decapitated a zombie with that axe and looked into the eyes of his wolf without fear.

She'd told him that he was beautiful.

Beautiful. In full hearing of his entire squad. He was never going to live the indignity down. Despite all that, Jack's lips curved affectionately as he followed Lillian along the narrow trail as it led deeper into the forest.

She'd proven her worth again. When they were trapped, she'd given them a way out. Abandoned maintenance tunnels underneath the hospital had allowed them to leave unnoticed by the gunships still circling lazily overhead.

Now they were deep in the woods and heading deeper into the forests that covered the mountains. Once in the wilds, they had half a chance of escape, and with them gone from the hospital, there was no need for the Project to bother with the hospital anymore. He knew them of old. Once they'd ascertained the wolves were gone, they'd level the south wing and anything left in there.

Walking behind her, he tried not to notice the delectable shape of her backside. She was delicate and feminine and so brave it humbled him, rocked him to the core.

She stumbled, but he was there in a heartbeat, his hand on her arm to help her keep her balance. She shot him a smile, but he recognized the strain there. The dark circles under her eyes told the rest of the tale—she was exhausted.

"Come here, sweetheart."

Ignoring her protests, he swung her up into his arms. With only the smallest struggle, she sighed and nestled against his shoulder. Deep within, his wolf rumbled approval. He had to agree with it. She felt right cradled against his heart. No matter what they'd done to him, how much of an animal they'd made him into, she'd seen right through it and into his soul. And she'd called him beautiful.

Looking down, he saw her eyes were already beginning to flutter closed. "That's it, sweetheart, sleep. I'll keep you safe."

The rest of the pack stopped when he did, the wolves silent as they automatically slid into cover. Only Darce approached, his paws soundless on the undergrowth.

"We need to go to ground. Work out our next move," Jack said quietly, careful not to wake the sleeping woman in his arms. "Less chance of us being made if we move at night. Send Nic and Sanders out to scout, find us somewhere to hole up."

She'd been asleep. Lillian jerked awake and looked around blearily, hoping to God she hadn't slobbered in her sleep. There was nothing more embarrassing than being out of it and drooling over your pillow, especially when there were people around to witness it.

The inside of a small bedroom met her eyes, the door half closed in front of her. Sitting up, she pushed the hair from her face and looked around. The last thing she remembered was being on the trail after they'd emerged from the tunnel. From there it had been a short hop to the outskirts of the woodlands that covered the hills around the hospital. She remembered the wolves around her. Some, like Jack, were in human form, but most of them flitted through the trees in their other form, as silent as shadows.

In all of it, bedrooms had not figured heavily. Rustic in design, it had to be one of the old trapper's cabins. Vacationers were always asking for directions in town, but she hadn't realized that there were any this far into the hills. Tossing the light blanket back, she shivered as her bare feet hit the cold floor. Murmured conversation from the door in front of her reached her ears, so she headed toward it.

Pulling the door open farther revealed a cozy little scene. The wolves were all crammed into the tiny cabin's main sitting area, jostling for space on the single sofa and all trying to get in front of the radiant heater. Without the door between her and them, the conversation became audible.

"Move over, you flea-bitten mutt."

"Fuck off, I was here first!"

"If you—"

"Yeah? You and whose army?"

The conversation quickly descended into chaos as the sitting area erupted into a sea of fighting bodies. She winced as the bones popped and cracked, signaling several of the combatants were shifting to take advantage of their alternative forms.

Over space on the sofa.

There was a roar, and a large, vaguely humanoid body flew over her head. Lillian ducked as it crashed into the wall behind her. The entire cabin rocked down to its foundations.

"Just *what* do you think you're playing at?"

The wolves froze. Eyes rolled toward her, even in mid-bite or punch. Sometimes both at the same time. Lillian put her hands on her hips and glared at them all as she would misbehaving patients in the common room.

"Well? I'm waiting. You...if you *dare* bite him I *will* tan your doggy hide. Are we clear?"

A pair of amber eyes beseeched her. She shook her head.

"Oh no, not working. I had a black lab for a pet. You got *nothing* on puppy-dog eyes."

There was a harrumph and a pair of vicious teeth clicked shut. Silence descended as she looked around the little tableau. With most of the wolves part shifted between human and wolf forms, it was a horror writer's dream scene. Lillian didn't bat an eyelash. She was obviously losing it now.

"Well? I'm waiting."

Slowly, they stood, shifting back until there were four shame-faced men looking back at her.

"*He* started it."

"Did *not*."

"Did too. It's *my* sofa, I was here first!"

The fight threatened to kick off again, the two men in the middle, Thom and Blake if her memory served her correctly, pushing and shoving at each other again. She sighed. It was like the sandbox all over again.

"Don't you *dare* piss on the sofa. You can't mark it like territory," Blake snarled, taking another dig at Thom.

"*Whoa*! No one's pis...urinating anywhere. I don't know whose cabin this is, but it's not ours. So you'll use the toilet like adults or I'll put you all in diapers! And don't make the mistake of thinking I don't mean it!"

She glared at them until the uproar subsided. "I've had a

hell of a night. I've been attacked by a wacko doctor, zombies, and carted over the countryside. I am *not* in a good mood, so don't piss me off, understand?"

"Yes, ma'am."

She nodded. "Good. Now where's that boss of yours?"

"You looking for me, doll?"

Jack pushed off from the doorframe and strolled into the cabin. With a signal of his hand, he dismissed the rest of the squad, watching as they filed out of the door behind him. He wanted to be alone with Lillian. Finally.

At the sound of his voice, she turned and smiled. The expression took her from merely pretty to breathtaking. His gaze wandered over her, taking in every detail.

Fingers of late afternoon sunlight crept through the shuttered windows. They were surrounded by forest, but somehow it had found a way through to her. He smiled. She was a creature of the sun. The thin streams caressed her, making her pale skin glow and turning her dark hair into a warm, rich fall of curls.

She was a creature of light. Light to his darkness.

He moved toward her, trying for casual. There was nothing casual about his intent, though. She was his, and he intended to have her.

He saw the instant she registered the danger she was in. He would never hurt her, ever. It just wasn't in him. But her body was definitely in danger and, he hoped, her heart. Her breath caught, and her hand stole up to her throat as she took a step backward. He groaned as his wolf sat up and took notice.

"Don't run," he warned. "If you don't want this, tell me now. But don't run, don't ever run from me. Predators like to chase, sweetheart, and I'm the biggest predator around here."

She stopped moving. His wolf pouted. There was nothing the thing liked more than a good chase. He was all for it, especially if it ended with the two of them in bed, but that wasn't the way he wanted to claim his mate for the first time.

He took a deep breath, rolling her scent over his tongue. The fear there slammed his control back into place. Fast. She wasn't an animal, not like him. If he was honest with himself, she was way too good for him. He should let her go.

He couldn't. Not in a million years.

She stood her ground as he approached, just like she'd stood her ground with his men. He hadn't been able to believe his eyes when he'd walked in to find her scolding them like a bunch of kids. Totally unafraid, even though she'd seen exactly what they were.

"Good girl," he whispered as he stopped inches from her. So close he could feel a hint of her curves against his half-naked body. She bit her lip, and the darkness in her eyes nearly undid his control.

Reaching out, he traced a fingertip softly down her cheek. Her skin was smooth and fragrant. Despite the hard night, he could smell the faint trace of the floral perfume she'd used yesterday. She used strawberry shampoo and wore no hairspray. He smiled. He didn't like hairspray. It made him sneeze.

She tilted her head, baring her throat as he trailed his fingertips over it. A sensual submission so simple it stole his breath away.

"Lillian." Her name was a prayer and a demand rolled into one as he hauled her into his arms. He couldn't wait another moment to touch her and make her his.

Bending his head, he claimed her lips in the softest of

kisses. While everything male in him urged him to crush her to him and take what he wanted, he held it off. He wasn't an animal. He would do this properly. Like a man.

His lips whispered over hers, learning their shape and texture. The sharp bite of fear in her scent faded, leaving something warmer in its wake: the exotic, alluring aroma of her interest.

His large hand slid into her hair, curling around the silken locks to cup the back of her head and tilt it for better access to her lips. She shivered against him, a movement that had nothing to do with being cold. He smiled against her lips. She was his. He knew it, and she knew it.

Gently, he nibbled on her lower lip. His teeth were human-blunt, but even so, he couldn't risk breaking the skin and infecting her with the virus that lived within him. The medical bods had tried to explain it to him once. The virus could only take hold if he bit or scratched someone and it got injected directly into the bloodstream. It wouldn't kill her, but it *would* change her. He wouldn't do that, wouldn't take away her humanity like that.

She sucked a breath in, her lips parting on a tiny, sexy little noise that went straight to the already hard cock in his pants. He didn't waste the opportunity, gathering her closer still and dipping his tongue between her parted lips.

She tasted like sunshine and long, hot summer nights. Of everything he thought he'd lost when they'd made him what he was. Need and longing hit him hard. All he wanted to do was tear the clothes from her slender frame, tumble her to the floor and take her until she screamed his name.

Instead, he drew back and nibbled her lip again. She moaned in pleasure, the sound lost in his mouth and he felt like the most powerful man in the world. Repeating the move, he tried to get her to follow him, teasing her with his tongue until she growled in frustration. Her hands, which had been stroking over his shoulders and back, moved to cup the sides of his face as she kissed him back.

"You, sir, are a tease." Lillian broke away to complain. She looked up into bright, piercing blue eyes and tried to muster a smile. It was a half-hearted attempt. How could she smile when she felt like she'd been run over by a truck at Mach 1 and all she wanted to do was strip his combat pants from his delectable body and screw him until he begged for mercy?

His eyes twinkled with amusement and something else. Something hotter and darker that took her breath away. It drew her like a moth to the flame and, like that moth, she suspected she was going to get burned. Right now, though, she really didn't care.

She rose on her tiptoes to kiss him again. He held her so tight her breasts were mashed against his broad chest, the beaded pebbles of her nipples caught between them. They ached. Twin pulses of need that arrowed down to the throb building between her thighs.

She didn't know what had come over her. She'd never reacted to a guy like this before. Ever.

A suspicion forming in her mind, she pulled away to look up at him. "You haven't done anything freaky to me, have you? Like, you haven't got any weird pheromones making me act like a—"

She closed her mouth with a click. She had been going to say "slut". Color rose on her cheeks, burning so hot she could cook eggs.

He frowned and searched her eyes for a moment. A small smile curved his lips. He chuckled and shook his head.

"No, I don't have any freaky pheromones, sweetheart. What you're feeling is there because you *want* to feel it. Natural human reactions, that's all."

"Oh, good." She breathed a sigh of relief and looked up at him, abruptly a little shy.

"So...if I said I wanted to drag you into the bedroom back there and..." She swallowed her nerves, gathered her courage and blurted out, "...have sex until both of us were exhausted, what would you say?"

His nostrils flared as his expression tightened.

He shook his head. "I don't want to have sex with you, Lillian..."

A sickening feeling hit her low in the gut. *Oh my God.* Her heart thundered in her chest. Her vision grayed around the edges. Had she got the signals wrong? Had she just propositioned a man who was just kissing her to comfort her? Screw the eggs, her cheeks were hot enough to power a city. She should have kept her mouth shut.

"I want to make love to you. Slowly, completely, until all you think about is me. The pleasure I make you feel."

She couldn't speak. His words, the images her over-eager imagination fed her, short-circuited her brain. All she could do was nod dumbly and wrap her arms around his shoulders.

He didn't say anything else, just held her gaze with his. His eyes were forget-me-not blue, not amber. Tension stretched between them like an elastic band. Any moment now, it would snap.

Her hands smoothed over the hard muscles of his back. What would it be like to feel him moving over her, within her...? All that power and strength bent to pleasure instead of the pain these Project people had decreed. She only knew what he'd told her about them, but the phrase "sons of bitches" seemed more than apt.

"God, sweetheart, don't look at me like that," he groaned, leaning down and stealing another quick, hard kiss before sweeping her up into his arms.

"Why not? Like what?"

He shook his head, full lips quirking up. "You know what I mean, little minx," he said as he carried her through into the bedroom and kicked the door shut behind them.

Chapter Sixteen

He carried her easily, even though Lillian knew she was no lightweight. She had too many curves and actually liked to eat rather than pick at her food and complain about the fat on a lettuce leaf. Jack was gorgeous, so why he was interested in her she didn't know, but she could see it on his face as he looked at her. He made her feel like the most beautiful woman in the world. For that alone, she'd walk through the fires of Hell.

His arms were like iron bands around her back and under her knees. She didn't bother worrying whether she was too heavy. He wasn't human. She might have finally tipped over the edge into madness, but that little fact didn't bother her anymore. In fact, the differences between them both thrilled and fascinated her.

Silence filled the room. There was no need for talk. Looks and touches were enough. He paused by the small bed and put her down, every curve pressing against the plains of his hard, muscled body. Her breath caught in anticipation and sensual excitement. All that power and control, hers to command.

His hands stayed lightly on her hips as she reached out to touch him. The world outside the closed door ceased to exist. For now, it was just the two of them in the little room, with the sun beating at the window and the smell of summer hanging in the air. Her lips pursed as she traced the scars over his skin.

Too many hurts, so much violence.

Leaning down, she kissed them one by one, as though she could kiss the hurts away. Under her lips, his skin was satin heat, his scent clean and earthy at the same time, like the forest after the rain. She moved down, the muscles beneath her kisses jumping when she reached his abdomen.

"Might want to be careful down there, sweetheart. Straying into dangerous territory." His soft chuckle was a little shaky as she neared his waistband.

The area below it was tented impressively, the heavy length of his erection pressing hard against the zipper. A wicked grin on her lips, Lillian shot him a look, then leaned down to plant a kiss against the fabric.

Jack swore, his hand finding its way into her hair. Emboldened by his reaction, she opened her mouth and grazed her teeth lightly over the head of his cock within the fabric.

"Fucking *hell.* You're killing me," he groaned as he tightened his fist in her hair to hold her in place. Not too tight, but enough that she could tell he was fighting to stay in control.

The devil on her shoulder couldn't leave it at that. It just couldn't. It would only be content with pushing this powerful man as far as she could and damn the consequences. Sliding to her knees, she started to unbutton the waistband of his pants.

He shifted, spreading his legs for better balance. The low rumble that escaped his chest was a mixture of pure torment and eager anticipation. The first button popped, then the second. By the third, his cock sprang free eagerly, as if it couldn't wait to be in her hands.

He was huge. Lillian swallowed nervously. She'd seen him before, but he looked bigger now. Worringly so. Her mind did a rapid rewind. Every time he'd held her, kissed her, he'd never pressed fully against her. Had he been worried about scaring her?

A huff escaped her throat. She wasn't that easily scared. Wrapping her hands around the thick, purple-headed shaft, she explored him with soft touches and strokes. He watched her, his eyes midnight with desire. She liked that, liked that he liked to watch. It spurred her on, encouraged her to do things she wouldn't have done otherwise.

Wouldn't have done otherwise? Hell, she was already out of her comfort zone and heading over the horizon. Not a prude by any stretch of the imagination, most of her sexual experiences had been with "safe" men. Men who undressed and folded their clothes as they went. Men who liked sex with the light off. In a bed. Once a week. Men she quickly got bored with, needing something else, needing something more.

Wrapped in her own little world, she leaned forward and licked him experimentally. Her tongue contacted the wide head of his shaft and his taste exploded on her tongue. Musky and salty-sweet, it wasn't unpleasant. In fact, she liked it, which couldn't be said for some of her previous partners.

Letting that thought drift away, she concentrated on what she was doing. Licking again with the flat of her tongue, she wrapped her lips around the flushed head of his cock. He gasped a strangled, choked-off sound as she hummed in pleasure and amusement.

She smiled around him and slid him deeper into the warm wetness of her mouth. He tasted good, and although she'd never been particularly fond of this act before, she was developing a new appreciation for it.

"Oh God, sweetheart. That feels so good."

Jack held her hair lightly. Not to control her but, she suspected, more to have something to hold on to and ground himself with. Feminine satisfaction ran through her. She loved that he was so gentle even though his body trembled as he held still. She loved the fact she had this power over him, even though he could easily snap her in two if he wanted.

His cock jerked under her hands and lips, the big vein on the underside of the shaft pulsing. A drop of pre-come leaked from the slit at the tip. She lapped it up eagerly. A tortured groan left his lips as she took her time about it, and he pulled away.

"I'm sorry, sweetheart. I won't last long enough like that," he whispered as she pouted. His hand still in her hair, he urged her to her feet and backward onto the bed. "And I have far more I want to do to you, and with you, before that happens."

They fell onto the bed together, a tangle of limbs as he rolled over her. His fingers looped around her wrists, and he pulled them over her head, pinning her in sensual slavery under his hard body. She arched her back and pressed her breasts against the solidly muscled expanse. They ached, she ached, her pussy ached…an ache she knew instinctively only he could ease.

"You're wearing way too many clothes," he breathed by her ear, then paid homage to it, nibbling along the edge before pulling the lobe into his mouth and suckling. His tongue played with the tiny gold loop she wore, the flickering motion shooting hot and cold chills through her body.

"Then take them off," she panted, baring her neck. She needed more. More of his kisses, more of everything he was doing…more of him.

He chuckled, the sound a rumble against the tender skin of her throat. "Bossy little minx, but who I am to argue?"

The question was rhetorical, so Lillian didn't bother to reply. His large hands moved over her with a speed that spoke of desperation, and an efficiency that said he knew his way around women's clothing.

Somehow, she didn't think he was a cross-dresser.

"Done this a few times before, huh?"

She arched an eyebrow at him as he unsnapped her pants and yanked them down her legs. Her blouse was just as swiftly whipped up over her head.

He sat back on his knees and looked down at her. Lillian shivered at the heat in his gaze, like a blue inferno. Suddenly she was pleased she'd worn something pretty for work. Floral satin, the pattern tiny and delicate, covered her breasts, and the tiny thong made her feel that little bit naughty. Even though she didn't have a boyfriend, she liked expensive lingerie, liked the feel and sensuality of it against her skin.

Correction, she *hadn't* had a boyfriend.

Although...was boyfriend the right word to use for the man looming over her with carnal intent in his gaze? It was far too benign and nice a word for the heat that licked at her skin and dampened the lace between her thighs.

His nostrils flared and his eyes darkened another notch, until she was looking into midnight velvet. The humor died away as he leaned down and drew a line from her lips, all the way down her body with his fingertips. He traced the deep cleavage between her breasts and onward, down over her stomach until he reached the lace of her thong.

Sliding a finger under the tie on one side, he pulled it down, inch by slow inch. He didn't speak as his other hand joined the first in a mirror image, hooking under the lace and satin. She swallowed as the panties slipped down over her hips, her thighs. The lace between her legs peeled away, as though he were unwrapping a birthday present, to reveal the neat, dark triangle of clipped hair that covered her mons.

"Perfect."

His voice was so soft she wasn't sure she heard him properly, until he repeated himself. "Absolutely perfect."

He pulled the thong free, the satin skimming over her legs and feet to hit the floor somewhere behind him. His large hands wrapped around her delicate ankles and urged her legs apart. Soundlessly she obeyed, transfixed by the feral look on his face.

He was going to...oh God, he was.

Her eyes fluttered closed, unable to process anything but the feel of his lips across her skin as he kissed his way back up the inside of her leg. He paused for a second to flirt with the back of her knee, but soon moved on again and blazed a trail of kisses over her inner thigh. His broad shoulders forced her legs wider.

Even though the room was warm, being completely open as she was meant her pussy was exposed. A shiver rolled through her as a slight breeze of cooler air from the window washed over her lips and teased at her clit.

"More than perfect—amazing."

His voice was reverent. She bit her lip as his warm breath replaced the cooler breeze. Everything within her narrowed down to the ache between her legs and his next movement. Anticipation roared unchecked. Time slowed as she waited.

He brushed his tongue over her, and she nearly came off the bed. Pleasure cascaded as he circled her clit once and latched on, drawing the little bud of pleasure into his mouth to suckle on it. He sucked, nibbled and licked, concentrating on the tiny button of flesh. He didn't let up, driving her higher and higher with his lips and tongue until she couldn't breathe. She needed to come. Needed it so much that she was going to go insane with wanting.

Broken whimpers and pants filled the room. Belatedly, Lillian realized they were hers. Her hands twisted and tormented the sheets on the small bed as Jack gorged himself on his sensual feast.

"Oh...oh my God, I'm coming," she gasped, tapping at his arm as he cupped her breast through the lace. A silent signal for him to stop. Her previous boyfriend had always wanted her to wait to come until he was in her. Since it took him under a minute to finish, sometimes she had to get the timing right, or the main event was done and dusted before she got into her groove again. She'd made up for the loss with a large collection of vibrators.

Jack didn't stop. Instead, he growled and continued to feast, lashing her over-sensitive clit with his tongue until she screamed and shattered around him. Pleasure hit her hard, a blitzkrieg of sensation that left her breathless as it rolled through and around her. Jack thrust his tongue deep inside her, tongue-fucking her as she spasmed and stretched the feeling out until she was weak with the force of it.

"Oh my. That was..."

He pulled away as the last tremors rolled through her and crawled up her body. His long fingers hooked into the front of her bra and released the heavy fullness of her breasts to his hot gaze and hotter lips.

"Amazing. Simply amazing. You're amazing," he finished for her, his hair-roughened thighs brushing against hers. The bed shifted as he dipped his hips and fit the broad head of his cock against the slick wet lips of her pussy.

She bit her lip again as he slipped half an inch into her without pushing. She was so wet...she'd never been this wet for anyone before.

"Please," she murmured, and lifted her hips in invitation. He slid another few inches, and her body stretched around him.

With a mingled groan of need and feral possession, he

pushed into her all the way. It was a long, hot ride of pleasure as his thick cock stroked every nerve ending in her sensitive feminine sheath. Finally his hips met hers, his cock kissed the entrance to her womb and she had to try and remember how to breathe.

"God, you're tight. I've never felt anything so wonderful before."

He braced himself on one forearm, planted in the sheets next to her head. Holding his body rigid, he closed his eyes. She gripped his upper-arms as she waited for the slightly uncomfortable, full feeling to fade. She felt stretched, stuffed beyond capacity, and it burned.

It shouldn't hurt. It wasn't like she was a virgin or anything. Frustrated beyond measure, she shifted to try and get more comfortable.

"Ohhhhh..."

The moan of pleasure was torn from her lips as the slight movement stroked those nerve endings again, all at once. The burning disappeared, leaving her with just the full feeling and an irresistible need to move.

She did. She rolled her hips again. Jack swore, his cock swelling even further as it jerked inside her.

"Sorry, sweetheart, this isn't going to take long," he apologized, kissing her as he started to move. Long, slow pumps of his hips as he worked his thick cock in and out of her.

"I don't care. Just...just...faster."

She knew she was begging. She didn't do begging. Right now, she didn't care. She'd get down on her hands and knees and crawl over broken glass if he'd just keep doing what he was doing.

He groaned and increased his speed. The bed beneath them

squealed in protest, slamming against the wall rhythmically as he took her. With fast, heavy thrusts of his hips, he claimed her and made her his.

His lover. His woman... She felt the truth clean down to her soul as he drove into her.

Their movements got faster. Skin slapped on skin as the scent of sex and arousal filled the air around them like a fine perfume. Even though she'd just come, Lillian felt the familiar tightening between her thighs.

"That's it, baby, come for me again. I want to feel it, I want to come with you. Together," he whispered in her ear as she struggled to keep up with him.

It was there, the edge of the chasm. She screamed and fell willingly, pushed over as he slammed into her a last time and roared his own release.

She was in heaven. She'd come home.

Although he was sprawled on the bed, flat on his back with his arm around the slender woman at his side, Jack wasn't asleep. Far from it. Instead, he was in a comfortable cocoon. Not asleep, but a step from being truly awake. Ignoring the pull of full consciousness he lay, warm and comfortable.

He'd slept. Actually slept. The realization was one he was still trying to absorb as Lillian's evocative scent wrapped itself around him, ensuring he was just as trapped in her web as he had been hours ago when he'd finally claimed her as his mate.

He hadn't slept properly since the night he was turned. Most of the time he was like an insomniac on speed. As soon as it looked as though sleep would claim him, something...he had no idea what it was...kicked in and he was wide-awake. If he got an hour or two snatched here or there, then he'd had a good night.

Part of him desperately missed sleep, missed those lazy weekend mornings when the world consisted of little more than a soft mattress, a warm duvet and the blessed knowledge that he had nothing pressing to do or anywhere he needed to be until he reported back for duty on Monday morning.

However, another part of him rejoiced, if that was the right word. His life had changed. People who slept put themselves in danger. Any moment, Project heavies could burst through the door with tranq guns and silver chains, or worse, shove a newly turned Lycan through the door instead. Jack wasn't sure which was worse—the heavies meant another long spell enduring tests and the second option meant he and his pack had to subdue an often wild, usually terrified wolf. Sometimes they were too far gone into the madness and fear. He didn't like those. It meant a brutal and painful death under another wolf's claws. Usually his. He was pack alpha, it was his responsibility. He wouldn't put that on his men.

So he was always watchful, he was always vigilant and he was always waiting for the Project to try something.

That made the fact that he'd fallen asleep wrapped around Lillian all the more surprising. He'd have thought he'd be more protective, more watchful, now he had a mate to look after, rather than fallen asleep like a babe in arms.

She lay draped half across him, using his chest as a pillow. Her hair covered him like a blanket. The soft whisper of her breath caressed his chest and stirred the slight line of hair down the middle. In a lazy movement, he lifted his hand and tangled it in the long dark locks as a smile crept across his lips.

Memories of having her under him, around him, rose sharp and immediate. His cock was already hard, ready and raring to go. It was like she tapped into all the primal male aspects of his psyche and brought them out to play.

He didn't get it. Even before he was turned, he'd been strictly a "wham, bam, thank you, ma'am" type. Not the touchy-feely type, and not the type for a long term relationship. He could be called away at a moment's notice and be gone for months, so it had never seemed fair to ask a woman to wait around on the off-chance he might make it back. He'd never felt this way with a woman before. Never felt this need to cuddle up and wrap himself around her. To make sure every guy, human or wolf, knew she that she belonged to him.

Taking a deep breath, he pulled her scent into his lungs. So deeply down inside that she became a part of him. His wolf, usually close to the surface and ready for a fight, stirred lazily and then went right back to sleep. Damn idle creature.

The ever-present smile widened some more as he let the wolf sleep. If there was danger, he'd be off the bed in a heartbeat, the creature inside fully awake and both of them ready to fight to the death to protect their mate.

What was it about her? What made him feel this way? It wasn't protection. She was human, she couldn't fight her way out of a paper bag and the idea of Little Red Riding Hood protecting the Big Bad Wolf was ludicrous.

Clearing his mind, he concentrated, filling his senses with everything about the woman lying over him. The sound of her heart filled his ears, the soft whoosh of her breathing, the siren call of her scent filled his world.

It was her, just her, he finally decided. Something about her pulled him in, triggered something deep within and had its hooks into his soul. His arms tightened around her slender form and he knew that he'd go to the ends of the earth for her. He'd lay down his life in an instant to protect her, and if anyone ever threatened her...

The snarl rumbled up through his chest unbidden, nearly escaping from his lips. With iron control, he forced it back down. If anyone threatened her, then they'd better have a king's ransom in silver bullets handy, because he'd rip them limb from limb and dance in their scattered entrails.

She murmured, a frown on her face, as though she could sense his mood even in sleep. Her delicate hand fluttered against the toned muscles of his abdomen. A soothing movement.

Releasing a sigh of pent-up emotion over a threat that currently was only imagined, Jack dropped his head back to the soft pillows and studied the ceiling. They were in no danger. They'd escaped the trap at the hospital. He knew the Project—they would regroup and send more teams out, but that would take time. Before that happened, they would be gone. So there was no need to worry, but now that sleep had finally fled, he was wide-awake.

His gaze wandered over the ceiling. Wooden cladding covered it, the same as the walls. Light, dimming now as twilight approached, filtered in through the shuttered window above the bed. He liked the room; it screamed old-country rustic.

It was also highly defendable, with its small window and solid door. The soldier in him appreciated such things. The wolf in him was drawn to the link with nature, the fact that everything about them had once been part of something living, unlike the steel and concrete of their barracks back on base.

Jack snorted to himself. Barracks. Yeah, right. They might have been at one point, a couple of decades ago. Now they were little more than the shells of buildings ringed with reinforced girders and steel mesh. Oversized dog pens. They were lucky they had Richards in the squad. He'd been a plumber before joining up, a skill he'd never expected to have to use in the army. He'd managed to keep the toilets and showers working. Otherwise they'd have been pissing on newspaper in the corners like common mutts.

His heightened senses warned him a second before someone rapped on the door. He tensed, his body ready for a fight. The door slid open a few inches, and Jack was on his feet, stark naked and with a warning growl low in his throat.

The door stopped. He strode forward and threw it open to reveal a startled Sanders. The wolf's gaze flicked over Jack, over his broad shoulders before doing a quick dance down his naked body. When it reached his groin, a flush burned across Sanders cheeks, and he quickly found somewhere else to look.

Belatedly Jack realized giving the only gay wolf in the pack an eyeful wasn't the best, or most sensitive, idea he'd had all day. They'd left most of the homophobic crap behind with their humanity, but that didn't mean Sanders was going to find it easier to find a partner. The rest of the wolves in the pack were as hetero as they came, aggressively so.

"What's up?" Jack grabbed his pants and stuck his feet in the legs before dragging them up to cover himself.

"We're changing watch, boss. LT said to wake you, see if you wanted in."

Jack zipped the pants up with a swift movement and looked up. Just in time to catch the wistful look on the other man's face as he looked at the sleeping form of Lillian in the bed. His wolf didn't react, recognizing Sander's longing for a mate of his own, not for Lillian. His voice was soft when he spoke.

"It'll happen, Joe." He ushered the smaller man out of the room and closed the door behind them. "One day you'll find a guy who just can't resist you."

Sanders sighed as his gaze darted across the room. It was subtle, almost not there at all, but Jack caught it. For a split second, Sanders's face was wide open, his expression twisted with longing and need, as he looked over at the half-naked form of the pack's former plumber, Richards.

"Yeah, I know. But will he measure up?"

Heart wringing in sympathy, Jack dropped a hand on Joe's shoulder and squeezed. He'd never suffered the agony of unrequited love, but he knew it when he saw it. "Of course he will. More than. You'll see."

Chapter Seventeen

It was getting dark, the pale half-light of the advancing evening darkening to full night. Perched high in the branches of a tree, Antonia was nothing but a shadow among myriad others as she looked down on the small cabin.

The wolves had led her a merry chase, first through the unknown tunnel and then through the woodlands beyond. She had their scent, though, and there was nothing more tenacious than a vampire tracking its prey.

They'd been clever, or thought they were, by passing through running water. Since the scent she tracked was less about a smell and more about a psychic impression, they'd just gotten wet for no reason. Unless, of course, they were just trying to turn her stomach with the smell of wet dog. So far, it was working.

She was motionless, unless the movement of the branches as the tree swayed slightly in the breeze could be counted. Her black-on-black eyes tracked the slight movements of the wolves as they patrolled below her. They hadn't seen her. No surprise. She wouldn't be seen unless she wanted to be. Watching carefully, she finally moved and pressed the strip of plastic around her throat against her skin.

"Beta team, come up slowly on the right flank. Wolf patrolling south to north. Slow, that's it."

Her voice was almost inaudible, the mic picking up the smallest murmur, and her psychic net canceled out the rest. It was a combo that allowed her to get close into a situation and direct the rest of her troops in. Something the Project had hoped to capitalize on.

Cool idea, apart from the fact Antonia had been the only Blood who'd shown the ability. The rest were more into charging in and ripping throats out. Noisily. Fitzgerald had been pissed. Demanded to know why she could do it and they couldn't. It had taken all the self-control she had not to tell him it was the numb-nuts he was turning. More brawn than brains, so how could he expect them to show any kind of common sense or tactical ability?

One thought of the asshole in charge of the base brought a legion more. The conversation they'd had just before she'd set off in pursuit of the Lycans was still fresh in her mind.

"They're working as a pack, in both human and Lycan form."

Arrogant bastard had laughed, not believing her. "I'm sure you think they are, Major. But plenty of highly intelligent scientists assure me that they haven't evolved that far yet."

"They got an explanation for why when half the Lycans cut down the RAs we sent in with automatic fire, three of them ripped in with claws and teeth?" she asked, her voice as calm and sweet as she could make it.

That was the trick when dealing with assholes like Fitzgerald. A whole heaping of sickly sweet with a side of dumb, innocent blonde. Not that she *was* blonde, but that wasn't the point.

The silence on the other end of the line was telling. She waited and smiled as whispered mutterings replaced the silence. Sound didn't carry so well over phone lines, especially the old cables in place on the base. No high-tech lines, no cable link. Didn't want some enterprising little hacker to trick his way in and find out just how corrupt Aladdin's cave really was.

Finally, Fitzgerald came back on the line. "Are they part-shifting as well?" he asked, trying to sound knowledgeable.

Her lips quirked. She knew full well he had an egghead at his side, directing his questions. Changing position soundlessly, she scanned the area under her perch again. To her left, not a hundred yards away, sat one of the Lycans.

To the uninformed, he just looked like a freakishly large wolf, something that would inspire nightmares for years to come if any human hunter out and about in the forest were to come face to face with him. So far, though, they all looked like normal wolves, just bigger. She hadn't seen any Hollywood horror movie specials yet.

"Don't think so. Just one or the other, human or furry. Why?"

"Doesn't matter. Major, I'm ordering you to bring one in. Alive. Whatever the cost. Do you understand me?"

If the tone wasn't enough to make her freeze, the words were. Her agile mind analyzed the words and the situation within a heartbeat. This operation had been a strictly "no survivors, torch the place" kind of clean up. Now with evidence the Lycans were displaying new abilities, suddenly Full Bird Fitz was more interested.

Although Lycans and Bloods wouldn't get along if they were the last two species left on Earth, she didn't want to hand them over to the sadistic base commander. Whatever abilities they'd evolved and managed to hide, it gave them more of a fighting chance against their common enemy. One she was loathe to take away from them.

"Did you hear me, Major?" Fitzgerald's voice was sharp,

irritated. He didn't like being kept waiting. A total contrast to Garry, whose reserves of patience Antonia had never worn out.

"Yes, I heard." She sat for a moment, thinking. "With the resources at my disposal, I don't believe I can bring a subject in. Not alive."

It was a line lifted straight from the "how to be a prick to a superior officer" manual, but she didn't care. The guy was an ass, and she had no incentive to try and take any of the wolves alive. She liked her skin in one piece too much for that.

"Bullshit. Try." The growl was an order.

She sighed, about to close the line when he spoke again, this time as though the words were dragged from him. "Bring one in, alive, and there's something in it for you."

Curiouser and curiouser.

"Oh?"

"Maybe...it's not been tested yet, mind you...but there may be a cure for your...condition."

A cure. Just the thought had held her spellbound for long moments after Fitzgerald had cut the connection. She'd never heard of a cure, for any of them. For re-animates, it was a no-brainer. The RA17 virus killed them dead and then piggybacked on their decaying bodies. Garry had been the only one she'd ever seen display any sign of memory or intelligence.

The thought of her dead friend snapped her out of her reverie. She might never have considered him such when he lived, but she was claiming the relationship now. He needed someone on the inside to avenge him.

Something inside her rebelled. Since her turning, she'd acted like the dead thing she thought she'd become, refusing any and all overtures of friendship until there was no one and nothing she held close.

Fitzgerald was a lying bastard at the best of times. She frowned, the crease in her brow the only movement she made. Did she dare take the risk, though? What if he actually was telling the truth this time, and there was a cure?

Her hand stole back up to her throat, her slender finger finding the depressions to activate the microphone. “Close the net at the back. Let’s hunt us some wolf.”

Lillian woke to an empty bed with sheets that smelled of Jack. Rolling onto her stomach, she wrapped them around her and smiled in contentment. Erotic memories of the last few hours filtered through her semi-doze. Her body ached in places she hadn’t thought of for months, certainly not since she’d split with her last boyfriend. It ached in other places she’d had no idea even existed.

Her smile grew until she was sure she resembled the cat that got the cream. For all his roughness and other problems, like the fact he wasn’t human, as a lover he was thorough and inventive. Dominant and gentle by turns, he was...wow. Just wow.

She didn’t have the words in her head to describe him, so she gave up and just giggled instead and dragged the pillow over her head. Lillian was not a giggler, but this time she couldn’t help it. The happy feeling inside bubbled up and over like champagne, released in sound.

Pulling the pillow away, she looked at the ceiling and wondered when he’d be back. The sheets beside her were cool, indicating he’d been gone a while. Disappointment filled her. She wanted his arms around her again.

She wriggled from the embrace of the sheets and looked about for her clothes. Luckily, Jack wasn’t a clothes flinger, so she didn't have to recover her panties from a lightshade.

Grimacing, she pulled her clothes on and headed for the door. She needed a shower or a bath. There were too many hours between her and hot water, not to mention a zombie attack, a mad dash through a tunnel and a hot sex session with the man of her dreams.

Was he, though...? Was he the man of her dreams, or had she fallen prey to some twisted version of Stockholm syndrome? Putting the thought out of her head, she stepped into the main room.

It was dark and empty. Surprise filled her, and a dead weight settled in her stomach like a brick. After everything, had Jack just up and left her here to fend for herself? She couldn't make herself believe it, but standing in the middle of the deserted main room, it looked as if she had no choice. She didn't blame them if they had. She was just human, a liability. She'd slow them down, and without her, they'd be able to cover more ground faster.

Her heart twisted as she walked through the empty room aimlessly. It took less than a minute. With nothing else to do she sat on the edge of the sofa, and pushed the hair back from her face. She should go, head back to the hospital. They'd be worried about her. Probably thought she was dead.

An aching sense of loss filled her and she looked around the room without seeing it at all. For weeks...months even...she'd been complaining to her friends that her life was too boring, too humdrum. Out of nowhere, Jack and his men had crashed into her life. Suddenly, for the space of a few hours, she was part of something bigger. Something out of the ordinary, fantastical and wondrous in a gory way. She'd been a player, admittedly a minor one, in a story straight out of Hollywood or a *New York Times* bestseller.

Like fairy dust, or pixie gold that disappeared with the rays of the morning sun, it was over. She'd been found wanting and left behind. Rubbing her hands over her face, she fought the hot prickle of tears as they stabbed at the back of her eyes.

She would not cry. How pathetic was that? She was her own woman, not defined by a man. And she certainly wasn't going to become a blubbering mess because one had decided she wasn't worth the effort. Even if the bastard had decided to screw her before he disappeared. A bitter smile twisted her lips. Oh well, at least he was true to male form.

The sound of a toilet flushing in the cabin somewhere behind her made her jump. She turned just as Darce stepped out of what must be the bathroom. She'd never been so pleased to see anyone in her life. They hadn't left her!

"Hiya. Was beginning to think you'd all abandoned me." She smiled and waved a little, self-conciously. Darce looked up, his eyes human-hazel under the dark bangs of his long hair. He smiled as soon as he saw her, his lips curving broadly. Easygoing and with an aura of enthusiasm, he was an easy person to like. She'd seen him battle his beast and control it, so she knew she could trust him. Perhaps as much as Jack. Probably why he was the pack second in command.

"Heya, gorgeous. No, not at all. The rest are out on watch"

Naked to the waist, he wore the combat pants she'd seen him in earlier, now grubby and stained on one leg. She didn't ask what the stain was. She had a feeling she didn't want to know.

"Don't you guys get cold feet?" she couldn't help asking as she noted his bare toes peeking out from under the pants leg.

A low chuckle rumbled around the room, the buzz in her ears telling Lillian most of the sound was outside her hearing range. Outside any human's hearing range.

"Nope."

He moved past her to the window. Standing to one side, he twitched the curtain and checked outside. Whatever he saw out there made him relax, the slight tension she hadn't been aware of leaving his broad shoulders. Within seconds, it was back again as his gaze settled on the window opposite.

"Most of us would still be running about half naked in the middle of the Arctic. Apart from Nic—she gets cold easy. Bizarre, if you ask me. She's got the coloring of a snow wolf, but she bitches at the slightest bit of cold."

Lillian padded after him on bare feet as he moved from window to window, checking. She tried to move up alongside him to see what he was looking for, but he blocked her with his larger body.

"Sorry, chick, eyes only. I can take a bullet and survive, you can't. And Jack'll have my guts for garters if you so much as break a nail."

She pulled a fake pout and laughed when he rolled his eyes at her. Twelve hours ago, she didn't know him from Adam, but he was so easygoing it was like talking to her brother. If she had one, which she didn't, but it was exactly how she'd have expected to treat her brother if she did.

"What're you looking for?"

A frown creased his brow as he moved back to the first window again. Again with the curtain twitch and the serious look as he peered out into the darkness.

"I don't know. Something feels...odd."

She lifted an eyebrow. "Odd how? We're in the cabin in the middle of the woods after the zombieclypse at the hospital. You're a werewolf. There are more werewolves out there. I'd say odd is a relative term, wouldn't you?"

He blinked, laughed and dropped the curtain.

"You're right, I'm being stupid. But...you know that odd feeling you get when someone's watching you, or you catch something out of the corner of your eye?"

She nodded. It was a feeling she had often. Mostly she put it down to working in a place with such a wealth of history. The amount of time St. Mary's had been a hospital, there were bound to be a few ghosts around the place.

He sighed in frustration and flicked the curtain down again. Leaning against the wall by the door, he ran a hand through his long hair. The ends just brushed his bare shoulders. His very broad and very lickable bare shoulders. But however nice-looking she thought he was, there was no spark of interest within her. Good thing, really. If there had been, she would have been as dumbstruck by his bare chest as she was when Jack was around.

"It's not just that, though," he carried on, his expression drawn. "It's a scent as well. Like a hint of perfume on the air after a woman walks from the room. Warm, like it's only just left her skin. But when I try and isolate it, it's gone."

She edged back on the sofa and curled her feet up under her. It was warm in the room thanks to the small heater, so she didn't need the blanket lying across the back of the sofa.

"My perfume, perhaps?" she offered. "I didn't think it was that strong, but perhaps you're getting a hint of that."

Darce shook his head. "I can tell the difference. And besides, you're not wearing perfume anymore."

Lillian frowned and sniffed experimentally at her wrists. It was faint, but she could still smell the base notes of rose and sandalwood from the perfume she'd sprayed on after her shower yesterday.

"You got a cold or something? Because I am, I can smell it.

Here."

She held out her wrist to him to prove it. Darce's expression was pained as he shook his head. She got the feeling if he could have backed up, he would have.

"Sorry. Not what I meant. To us, you're not wearing perfume because we can't smell it. All I can smell on you is Jack."

"Jack?"

He nodded, his hair dancing over his shoulders again.

"Yeah. Since you...and he..." He whistled and slid one finger in and out of the circle of his thumb and forefinger on the other hand. "All I can smell is his scent. Mate-marking. It's so other wolves know you're taken."

He could smell Jack on her. A mate-mark. Oh God, why hadn't she thought of that? With such a sensitive sense of smell, he probably knew exactly what they'd been up to in the last couple of hours. *Well, durr...* the little voice in her head chided. *Wouldn't take a damn genius to work that one out with all the noise we were making.*

Lifting her head, she ignored the flush and went for flippant to cover her embarrassment. "Wait. You're saying I smell like wet dog?"

His head snapped up at the jibe, his lips parting to retort. Instead, his gaze shifted and went out of focus as though he was concentrating on something she couldn't see or hear.

Something about the set of his body, the intense focus, made her pause. Sent a shiver of warning through her body. Warily, she rose to her feet. "Lieutenant?"

"Fuck." The expletive exploded from him with the force of a small nuclear blast. "They're here. We gotta go."

The window behind him exploded, spewing glass into the

room and across the floor like candies from a broken piñata.

"Go!" he yelled, already across the room and shoving her toward the bedroom ahead of him.

She didn't argue. She just ran. Darce was hot on her heels as they crashed through the door of the bedroom. He slammed the door shut and wheeled around. Lillian's jaw hit the deck as he lifted the heavy wooden dresser and dragged it into place over the door as though it weighed nothing.

He turned to find her watching him. Something heavy slammed into the door behind him.

"Window."

He grabbed her hand, dragging her after him like a trailer on tow as he ran over the soft surface of the bed. The window didn't stand a chance against however many pounds of determined werewolf, the glass shattering in a discordant aria. Her heart slammed in her chest, a painful tattoo as she clambered through the ruined opening. Not quickly enough for Darce, though.

"Sorry, chick. We gotta haul ass."

His apology was short as he grabbed her bodily. She gasped as her feet left the ground. The next instant her world narrowed down to a close-up view of naked werewolf back and a tight ass pumping away just below her. Holding her tight over his shoulder, Darce ran.

Shouts and gunshots rang around them. Howls of warning and rage filled the night air. Fear locked her muscles as she clung to her rescuer to avoid being thrown off. She locked down the little voice in her head that was screaming about being the pathetic female in need of rescuing.

Darce was a werewolf. He was stronger and faster than her. If he felt the need to get her out of a danger, then she wasn't exactly going to refuse. What were her choices, anyway? She could either let him manhandle her or complain and waste time. Or get killed. None of those options, particularly the last, appealed.

The world became a frightening place. Darce ran through the blackened forest with her across his shoulder like some kind of freakish lump. With each shot that whistled by them, she winced. Each time he leaped over something in their path, she flinched. As a teenager, she'd always loved roller coasters, rides that got the heart pumping and the adrenalin running. Now she was on the ultimate thrill ride as they ran for their lives, and all she wanted was for it to stop.

The gunfire slowed, petered out behind them as the humans chasing them couldn't keep up. Darce crashed through another clump of trees and came to a stop. As soon as her whirling senses told her they were stationary, she wriggled.

"Put me down. I can run," she promised, but he was already sliding her down from his body to the floor. Unlike with Jack, the movement wasn't sensual. His body was hard and comforting in its strength. Even though he was built as nicely as his boss, there was no answering spark within her. It was as though that switch had been flipped and the only guy she'd ever respond to again was Jack.

Darce stood motionless, his head cocked to the side as though he was listened to something. She tried to do her best not to breath so he could hear better. The forest was silent, mocking her own attempts at listening. She couldn't hear shooting or howling anymore.

Her gut twisted. Had they killed all the wolves...? *Oh my God, please let Jack be okay.*

"They're still out there. Following us." His voice was a low murmur. "We're on silent running now. No vocal warnings until we RV."

"RV?"

"Rendezvous. Standard protocol. If the shit hits the fan, we cut loose and make our way to a pre-defined location," he explained, looking up. He nodded toward the mountains to their left. "If we get split up, head parallel to those until you hit a road. Follow it into the pass to the next town. Someone will find you."

Chapter Eighteen

The Lycan was with the woman, and *fuck* was he fast. Antonia swore under her breath as she followed their frantic flight through the night-darkened forest. Even carrying the woman didn't seem to be slowing him much, and Antonia struggled to keep up, despite the fact she wasn't carrying anything heavier than a pistol in a shoulder holster.

She'd ditched her rifle. It would only snarl her up as she travelled through the treetops far above the ground. Besides, she had natural weaponry, and they were far more effective than any bullet.

He pounded along the ground, moving low and fast. The woman's weight didn't seem to bother him. In fact, from his breathing and heart rate, Antonia suspected he hardly noticed the weight across his shoulders at all. He didn't slow his pace, not even to leap over fallen logs or to clamber up the rock formations that littered the forest floor like some giant child's discarded playthings.

She switched direction when he did, following the lee of the mountain range above. The trees were denser here, which slowed her down. Not much, but enough she had to expend more energy than she liked to boost her speed. More energy expenditure meant she burned through her resources quicker. She would have to feed before the night was out and, being this far from the base, that meant a live donor.

The obvious choices were the men under her command. Her lip curled. They were pumped full of shit to keep them from being infected, which meant their blood would taste...well, like shit. But unless she got lucky and came across a civilian camping out in the woods who'd somehow missed the firefight when they attacked the cabin or the numerous werewolves stampeding through the trees, then she had no option.

Unless... An image of being wrapped around the cute as all hell Lycan she was chasing popped into her head. His arms 'round her waist, hers across his shoulders as she bent his head to the side to bare his throat. The big vein pulsed under his tanned skin, calling to her. His amber eyes shone with lust and need as she bent her head, her fangs full and aching in her mouth—

No! That is so not fucking happening. Not in a month of Sundays. Ever. She shuddered and carried on moving, ignoring the heat that washed through her body. Lycans were filthy creatures, the lowest of the low. No way would she lower herself to drink from one. Even one as sexy as the Lycan she was chasing. Besides, she had enough crap going on with the virus already in her veins. She didn't need to add another to the mix, even for kicks and giggles.

Reaching a clearing, the pair below her stopped. Clinging to a branch, she stopped herself in the same instant. Her nails, elongated and razor sharp, bit deep into the bark. A silent shadow she watched what was going on underneath her branch. She wasn't worried they would look up and see her. If Lycan eyes couldn't distinguish her from the darkness, then a human had no chance. And the wind was the wrong way for him to catch her scent. She crept forward on her branch until it dipped under her weight.

"...someone will find you."

Find her? What was he going on about? She wished she'd caught the first part of the sentence. Was the wolf cutting the human woman loose or something? Out here in the darkness, miles from anywhere?

Wriggling, she gained another couple of inches. The wood beneath her creaked. Below her, the Lycan's head snapped up as, beside him, the woman drew closer. His eyes glowed amber-green as the light from the moon struck them. She froze.

He could see her. Instead of that preternatural gaze sweeping the shadows among the branches seeing just the darkness, he focused directly on her. Surprise was stark on his face.

"Go."

He pushed the human female away, detaching her hand from his arm and shoving her toward the small, barely visible track they'd been following. Antonia's lip curled back in a snarl, hatred and anger welling up inside her. What was the female doing near him, why was he touching her? Her talons retracted, freeing her from her perch. She dropped to the forest floor and landed in a crouch.

"Run. Now!" her Lycan bellowed at the human, his eyes not leaving Antonia's as he dropped into a fighting crouch. She scuttled to the side, trying to find a way around him. Instinct and rage rode her. Her gaze locked onto her target, the delicate woman behind the Lycan. She was pathetic, human and weak. Nothing like Antonia.

She wouldn't be able to defend herself, not against the claws and ferocity of a Blood's anger. Just one swipe of her extended claws and the woman's throat would be ruined, her lifeblood pouring from her veins. A low rumble left her throat. The human was a dead woman—she just didn't know it yet.

Their eyes locked, blood darkness against human warmth. The human gasped as she read her own death in Antonia's eyes. Her hand flew up to her throat as she stumbled backward. She almost fell, her feet slipping on the wet leaves underfoot.

"Run!"

The human did as she was told, triggering every predatory instinct within Antonia. All she wanted to do was run, chase her rival down and put her out of commission. The Lycan sidestepped, putting himself between Antonia and her prey. She snarled at him in fury, flashing her fangs.

"Now, now," he chided, shaking a finger at her. "Put them away unless you intend to use them, there's a good girl."

She wanted to rip that finger off and shove it where the sun didn't shine...she wanted to close in and lick it before sucking it between her lips, then watch the heat flare in his eyes. The urge to rip into him with claws and teeth warred with the need to throw him to the forest floor, tear his clothes from his body and ride him until they both screamed in pleasure.

She staggered, the internal battle tearing her in two. What the *fuck* was wrong with her? He was a Lycan, a freaking dog. A mutt she'd been ordered to put down. Or catch and muzzle.

"Get out of my way." Her words were low and guttural, the presence of full extended fangs in her mouth made speech difficult. "Or I'll rip your head off and dance in your entrails."

"Sure you will, sweetheart." He blew her a kiss, his words light and joking. "And I'll put you over my knee and spank that luscious backside of yours."

She snarled a wordless sound of anger and frustration. He beckoned her on, his eyes as hard as the amber stone they mimicked.

"Come on, gorgeous. Let's dance."

"Ohmigod, ohmigod, ohmigod."

The litany fell from Lillian's lips as she crashed blindly through the trees. Her sensible flats, more suited to walking the wards of St. Mary's than a mad dash through the woods, slipped on the wet leaves underfoot. Branches reached out grasping fingers to tug at her clothes.

Her heart pounded so hard it filled her hearing and competed with the harsh rasp of her breathing. Follow the mountains. She had to follow the mountains. The moon overhead disappeared behind a cloud. Panic clawed its way up her back as she was dropped into darkness. How could she follow the mountains when she couldn't *see* the freaking things?

She couldn't see, but she could hear. All around her, the once-silent forest erupted into a cacophony of noise, every little sound amplified and playing right into a fear of the dark she thought she'd left behind in childhood.

Every skitter of wind-blown leaves behind her was a zombie creeping up. Every creak of a branch above was one of those creatures dropping like death from above. A vampire...no, Blood...whatever the things were called. She shivered as she remembered the look on the woman's face. Rage and a soul-deep hatred she'd never expected to see in another person's eyes. Not directed at her anyway. She was a hospital manager, for heaven's sake. People didn't look at her as though they'd happily rip her limb from limb. Or if they did, they saved their ire for a complaints form.

The moon came out from its hiding place, the silvery glow illuminating the path ahead of her again. How Darce had seen where they were going, in the pitch black and at the speed he was going, she had no idea. It gave her a new appreciation for just how inhuman he and the others were.

"Oh, thank God."

She darted down the newly revealed path, her eyes wide as she scanned the woodlands either side of her. Just one glimpse of a furry hide was all she wanted. She didn't care which one of them she found, all Lillian wanted at the moment was the feeling of safety being near one of the werewolves gave her.

A hysterical snort escaped her as she rounded a corner and clambered over a fallen log. Her foot slipped again, and she lost precious seconds retrieving her shoe. What kind of twisted world had she fallen into where she looked to the creatures of nightmares for protection?

"Well, well. What do we have here?"

At the new voice she squeaked and shot upright, her wayward shoe clasped in one hand as an impromptu weapon. Not as effective as an axe for dispatching zombies, about all she would manage with the flat heel would be to spread its nose over its face.

*Durr...*zombies didn't speak and they certain didn't have the tonal range to manage lewd.

Standing in front of her was a soldier. At least, since he was dressed in black and carrying a rifle, she assumed he was a soldier. He had that vague military air about him that proclaimed him as such. Knowing her luck, she'd probably found the only soldier fan-boy serial killer in existence.

"Hello, sweetheart, going somewhere?"

She opened her mouth, intending to go for the "little woman in need of protection" act. Anything to get someone between her and the vampire in the darkness behind her. But the glitter in his eyes stopped her. There was no concern, just a predatory gleam in his pale blue eyes. Human or not, she knew in an instant she wasn't getting out of this alive. If he got hold of her, she'd wish for death long before it came.

Without thinking about it, she hurled the only weapon she had, her shoe, at him. Her aim was bang on. The slight heel hit him right in the nose. Blood splattered across his camouflaged skin, the scarlet vivid even in the silvery light of the moon.

"You bitch!"

She didn't wait around. Spinning on her heels, Lillian ran back the way she'd come. Her arms and legs pumped as she tried to put as much distance between her and the soldier she'd assaulted with a ballet flat as quickly as possible. Lillian Rosewood, master of origami and the ancient art of shoe-kung fu. Yeah right, she was so scared right now that if Bugs Bunny jumped out of the shadows in front of her, she'd shit herself.

Hitting a turn in the path, she slipped again but made it around. The heavy sound of booted feet thundered behind her. He was gaining, shouting threats as he ran. Looking around wildly, she tried to find somewhere to hide. He was human, not a wolf nor a vampire. If she could get out of sight, she had a chance.

Time was running out. She turned, still looking, her hair getting in her eyes. There, off the path. A huge broad trunk spilt by lightening, half of the wooden giant lying in state across the forest floor whilst the other reached majestically for the sky, as though unaware it was already dead.

Perfect. Her breathing rasped like a chainsaw in her ears as she raced through the undergrowth and scrambled under a loop of the fallen trunk. The warnings behind her got louder as she tucked herself into the charred hollow of the trunk and tried not to breathe. The gap was so small she felt as if she was in a coffin, her breasts squashed her knees. Breathing was bad; she might as well trumpet her location to the world.

"Come out, come out, wherever you are. Don't make me

find you. That'll just make me mad. You won't like me when I'm mad."

Why, asshole? Do you turn green and dumb...no, wait, you're already dumb. Despite her sarcastic thoughts, fear made it easy for her to keep quiet. Ignoring the burn in her legs, she didn't make a sound. Hidden from sight, sound was the only thing that would—

"Got you, bitch."

A hard hand closed around her arm. She screamed, fighting to stay concealed but he was too strong for her. The charred bark cut into the soft flesh of her knees, then snapped as he hauled her from her hiding place and into the open.

He wasn't alone. More shadowy figures surrounded her as he threw her to the ground and started to unbuckle his belt. "Now, let's have some fun, shall we?"

Chapter Nineteen

Darce felt his jaw drop, but couldn't do anything about it. She was beautiful. The epitome of feminine grace and lethality all wrapped up into one lithe yet curvy package that had his heart racing and his cock as stiff as an iron bar. Crouched in front of him, she was dressed for combat but looked nothing like any soldier he'd ever seen. Certainly none he'd ever served with heated his blood and tented his pants like this one did.

"Move out of the way."

Her voice was a melodious snarl, its dulcet tones stroking along the back of his neck as though it had fingers of its own. He wanted nothing more than to obey her, to step aside and let her pass. If he did that, though, Lillian's blood would be on his head. If that happened, Jack would rip his still-beating heart from his chest, and Darce really liked it where it was.

"Aww come on, doll. How about you stay and play a while?"

Watching her carefully, he took a step forward, then another. Adrenalin and wariness raced through his veins in tandem, a heady feeling. Baiting a Blood was like baiting a feral tiger. Dangerous as fuck.

It was the most fun he'd had in months.

"Forget the human. I'm much more fun, I promise."

Her eyes didn't leave him as he walked forward. Even if he

couldn't smell the difference in her scent, he would have known instantly from her stillness that she wasn't human. Humans didn't do "statue" very well, but Bloods managed it to perfection.

A hunting technique, the logical side of his brain informed him. The infection had hyper-evolved its victims into predators. Ones that preyed on humanity. The human eye was drawn to movement, so it stood to reason any creature hunting it could freeze at will. Like how she'd been hiding in the branches above them. Perfectly still, almost unseen, until her scent had given her away.

"I'll even roll over and let you rub my tummy, if you ask nicely."

Darce held his breath as he took another step. He was almost within range, just two more steps at the most, then it was game on. The murderous look in her eyes warned him that he couldn't let her get past him. Not that he intended to. Her scent wrapped around him and woke the beast inside. It growled and paced, not liking to be caged with their mate so close.

"I'll rip your fucking guts out."

She shifted back a pace, still watching him. He took a step forward. She was nervous of him. Good. Even though she was his mate, and he wanted nothing more than to wrap her in his arms and keep her safe from harm, Darce knew it wasn't going to be that easy. She was in blood lust, her eyes shining with a feral light as she looked past him the way Lillian had run.

He was going to have to beat the living snot out of her to break its spell.

"Why don't you come try?"

He stepped in, his arms spread wide in invitation. Every cell in his body tensed in anticipation of her attack. He didn't allow his gaze to drop from her eyes, but he knew the fingers coiled into the dirt beneath her weren't human anymore. He'd caught a glimpse of razor-sharp talons as she'd dropped from the branches above.

Their gazes locked, time stretched between them as tension grew. With the threat of violence, his vision sharpened and cast everything around him into high relief. The slightest movement drew his attention, the smallest sound. Power roared through his veins and the potential of his change crawled over his skin like a thousand ants.

She attacked without warning. Fast and low. He had barely enough time to block as one set of claws slashed at his face and the other toward his abdomen. Heat and pain drew lines across his forearms as her talons opened his skin like a hot knife through butter. Setting his teeth, he ignored it and broke away.

His joking demeanor fell away. She was fast. Faster than he'd thought.

"Not so cocky now, are you, sunshine?" A hint of amusement entered her eyes as she circled him. Graceful. Lethal. Like the big cats he'd admired as a child. Would she purr when he had her in his arms?

He shrugged. Blood ran down his arms and dripped from the ends of his fingers. He hadn't shifted. Not yet. The power coiled and writhed just under his skin. He held onto it despite the sting.

"I'm always cocky. It's part of my charm."

He didn't cup his crotch as he normally would or otherwise bring to her attention that he was hard. She might think he was some sick fuck who got off on violence. How could he explain to a Blood he was hard because she was his one and only? She'd tear his throat out first.

He turned as she moved, careful not to put his back to her.

She watched him, her stare as unflinching as a snake. He wondered what color her eyes had been before the change had stolen all the color from them.

She lunged again, testing his reactions. He blocked, but she was already moving. A whirling dervish of fists and feet. His heart pounded and his breath rasped. His world narrowed down to blocking her lethal strikes and trying to find a way past her defenses. Smaller and lighter, she could play chicken with a freight train if she wanted. But so could he. *Just one hit, that's all he needed.*

Talking was a thing of the past as the battle raged around the small clearing. The moon hung above them, its glare unimpeded as it lit the clearing like a spotlight. He twisted and turned, using everything he had as she worked away. Bloods were closer to the dead than Lycans were, but even so, he could see she was breathing as heavily as he was, the front of her uniform soaked in sweat and outlining her breasts.

His mind took a break, high-tailing it off into the land of fantasy and wet dreams as he imagined stripping the wet fabric from those luscious mounds. His mouth watered at the thought of sucking her erect nipples. They'd be small and perky...

She opened his cheek from eye to jaw.

"Pay attention, mutt."

Darce rocked back on his heels, his guard coming up a little bit too late as he waited for her to rain blows down on him. Damn it. He'd let his imagination get away with him. Let her scent affect him so much he took his eye off the ball. His irreverent sense of humor snickered deep inside. Wolf...Dog. Ball.

The attack never came. Instead, she wheeled away and paced around him as he recovered. He wiped a hand across his face. The line she'd drawn with her claws would scar. He could feel it already. Absurdly, he smiled, even though it hurt like a bitch, the edges of the wound puckering and burning. She'd marked him. Every day he'd look in the mirror and remember her.

"That all you got, doll?" He blew her a kiss. "I'm gonna think you're sweet on me. Or are they diluting down the stuff they use to make you guys these days?"

That did it. Rage filled her eyes, the deep black shining with red. He dropped to a defensive crouch, ready for anything, and suppressed a shudder. Red eyes. Man, that was some scary shit.

He barely had time to collect himself before she charged. This time, the game was on in earnest. She was a tsunami of anger and sheer skill. He couldn't keep up with the flurry of blows. No time for teasing her now. He traded witty comments for breathing, blocking for all he was worth as he tried to turn the tide of the battle. She worked him like a speed carver. Always chipping away, trying to get past his guard and reach his throat or the relative softness of his unprotected abdomen.

Change, change. Me, me, me! the wolf inside demanded. But he refused it, locking it within his human flesh. She was shit-fast and intelligent as hell. He needed all his human smarts. The wolf was fast, probably faster than she was, but he couldn't risk a shift and have her out-think him.

The flurry of blows continued. He had to let some through, grunting as they landed with bruising intensity, so he could throw his own. Her face drew tight with pain each time one landed. His heart ached. Pounding on his own mate? He was a shit.

He saw the opening. She slid to the side and pulled her arm back to deliver a blow that would rock his head on his neck but left her side unguarded. Quick as a snake, he slid into the gap and wrapped her up. He shoved his leg around hers, a big arm twining round her neck as he used his hip as a pivot point. He yanked. Rode her falling body to the floor and pinned her.

She fought like a wildcat. All sharp edges and hard knees. It was like riding a bucking bronco, but way more fun. He panted as he got a leg over both hers, bringing his groin flush against hers. Within seconds, he had her hands pinned above her head.

Even though there was no way out, she still fought him. Spitting fury she tried to wrench her hands away, the movement so violent he felt the bones beneath the delicate skin pop.

"Hey, hey…let it go, doll," he breathed against her ear. Her heart pounded almost as fast as a human heart, betraying her fear. If he felt a shit before, now he felt lower than shit. He was proto-shit. No, lower than that. Sub-shit. The lowest of the low.

"It's okay, I won't hurt you."

All movement beneath him stopped. He looked up and right into the dark wells of her eyes. The expression there nearly killed him. Loneliness, misery and fear warred with something else. The tiniest expression trying to break through like a plant struggling to grow in the middle of a concrete jungle. Hope…and longing.

Unable to help himself, he lowered his head and claimed her lips. Just the softest brush of his lips over hers.

She flinched at the touch, but didn't turn away. Just held still under him. Unmoving. *Slow*, he cautioned himself. He needed to seduce her senses and get her to open up to him. Her lips were like silk, soft and yielding with just a hint of something indefinable. Erotic and innocent at the same time. He knew from just one touch he'd never be able to get enough. He bit back a moan, resisting the urge to dominate and take what he wanted.

He nibbled at her lower lip, careful not to nip her even with his human-blunt teeth. She was a Blood, but that didn't mean she found biting sexy...and he couldn't afford to fall prey to stereotype in his battle to win her heart. The firm, uncompromising line of her lips started to soften as he continued his assault, molded to his, then started to cling. His heart sang. She wasn't indifferent to him. Behind her hesitant response, there were fires of passion. He just needed to coax them out.

Snick.

Darce froze at the small metallic sound behind him, his lips still on hers. The circle of a muzzle pressed against the back of his head, cold even through the cushion of his hair. Then it moved.

"Game over, handsome," the woman under him whispered as a blinding pain exploded on the side of his head, just above his ear. Then Darce knew no more.

The situation was FUBAR'd to hell and back. Jack stood outside the little cabin Sanders had found earlier, hidden deep in thicker trees and undergrowth, and looked about at the destruction. The door was off its hinges, the windows shattered. A curtain waved gently in the breeze, its bottom edge charred and ripped.

Lillian was gone.

"Who was with her?" His voice was tight as he fought for control. With the rotational watch, he didn't know which of the pack had been on duty in the cabin.

He didn't care which of the wolves milling about the

clearing answered him. He just needed to know.

Nic emerged from the ruined interior, in human form and as naked as the day she was born. Blood covered her slender figure, none of it her own. Jack didn't blink an eye. Clothes didn't survive the change, so nakedness was something they all had to accept quickly.

"Darce. They went out the back window."

Relief hit him hard and fast. Despite his words to his second-in-command earlier, Darce was just as capable a fighter as him. Probably better. Younger than Jack, he had a mean streak a mile wide under that joking exterior.

Dropping the soldier he held to die at his feet in spine shattering agony, Jack stepped over the shuddering form. He didn't care. The bastard and all his little friends could rot in hell for all he cared. They'd attacked the cabin with guns and explosives, knowing there was a defenseless woman in there.

Guns hadn't helped them when the wolves had fought back. The soldiers hadn't stood a chance. If they'd thought Lycans were dangerous before, the fact that a wolf-mate had been threatened, no matter whose, had brought out the beast in all of them. They'd stood even less chance afterwards.

The small amount of information the wolves had gleaned from the terrified soldiers indicated that Lillian had been collateral damage. Which meant the soldiers had thought to have a little fun with her. Now they were twisted and grotesque corpses littering the clearing around the cabin.

"Good."

The scream echoed through the trees. High-pitched, it was the sound of fear and pain. A woman's fear and pain. Jack's head snapped up, a feral snarl curling his lips. Lillian's voice. She was out there somewhere, hurt and scared. Someone was hurting his mate... He caught Nic's pale eyes. They reflected his horror and rage.

"We'll clean up." She jerked her head toward the sound of the screaming. "She needs you. *Go*!"

He didn't need to be told twice. He turned and ran. Taking three steps, he launched himself forward, changing in midair. His paws hit the ground, claws biting deep and driving him forward.

He ran like he'd never run before. He'd always loved the speed and agility of his wolf body, sometimes changing just for the thrill of running on four paws. For the exhilaration of pushing himself to see just how far and fast he could go.

There was no thrill and no enjoyment in his soul now. Speed was all that mattered. His heart thundered as his massive rib cage expanded to drag in more air, powering him forward ever faster. He twisted and turned, leaped over fallen logs and boulders alike, but saw none of it. Every second that passed was too much. Every second was another in which Lillian was being hurt or worse.

He lost her scent, but another scream spurred him on. Changing direction, he cut through the dense forest. He was close, so close he could hear male laughter and a woman's sobbing.

There. Just up ahead through the trees. Lillian on the ground, a soldier on top of her, trying to force her thighs apart. Her pants were torn, the fabric ripped from waist to crotch. Already her delicate skin darkened with the beginning of bruises.

Anger slammed through him, stealing his breath and replacing the energy in his veins with a tower of rage. They were hurting his mate. He would kill them all.

A red mist bathed everything he saw as he crashed into the clearing, morphing into a hideous half-man, half-beast. On two legs, he charged, ignoring the two other men to tackle the one on top of Lillian, taking him to the ground next to her. Rearing back, he swung. His claws ripped into the man's unprotected throat, tearing a gobbet of flesh free. His mate flinched as arterial blood sprayed her.

No time to see if she was okay. Leaving the dying man to choke his last, Jack jumped up on his misshapen feet. A rifle swung toward him. The finger attached to the trigger didn't get time to tighten. Jack took the arm off at the shoulder. A swipe of his claws ensured the human had more things to worry about as his guts spilled to the dirt at his feet.

He kept moving, his claws alternately flashing in the moonlight and dripping blood. In less than a minute, he'd rendered the clearing into an open-air slaughterhouse. Bits of bodies, not men, littered the forest floor. An arm or a leg was distinguishable, but the rest was pretty much chum.

Chest heaving, he closed his eyes and dropped his head back as he fought to control himself. There were no more enemies, no one else to kill. There was just him and Lillian left. Just the thought of her snapped him back into focus.

Lillian. Was she okay, had that guy hurt her?

He turned, his clawed foot breaking something underfoot. He looked down, expecting to see a twig. It was a human thighbone, de-fleshed, its blood-splattered ivory surface gleaming in the moonlight.

Abruptly, he felt sick. What must Lillian think of him? She was human, he was an animal. An animal that had torn three men literally to pieces in front of her…less than pieces. Most of the remains could double as butchers mince.

The sound of her unsteady breathing, thick with tears, reproached him. She was terrified, he could smell it on the air. Hesitantly, he approached her. She'd curled into a small ball, arms and legs close to her body, like a child trying to shut out a world too cruel to cope with.

How could he even think of being near her...of touching her after this, never mind anything else? He wasn't human. She was way too good for him and always would be. That he loved her, that his wolf howled at the mere thought of leaving her where she was on the forest floor, didn't matter. He may be an animal now...but there was just enough of the man left in him to walk away. Maybe.

Until she sniffled and lifted her head. A pale hand pushing her hair out of her face, she looked about. The pale skin of her face went green as she caught sight of the slaughter, but she quickly looked on, searching for something.

Him. Her dark gaze latched onto him. He fought the urge to step back, hide his hideous misshapen form in shadow. Any moment now he expected the dazed expression on her face to dissolve into horror and for her to start screaming again. His heart pounded, the fight or flight syndrome firmly switched to flight. He couldn't face her seeing him like this and turning away in disgust.

She didn't scream. Instead she scrambled to her feet and, in a move beyond his wildest dreams, launched herself into his arms.

"Oh my God, Jack. I thought you'd never come. They were...they..." Her voice cracked as she buried her face into the fur that covered his body and wrapped her arms as far around him as she could. Her petite frame shook with the force of her trembling. So hard he was surprised she didn't break her own teeth. He pulled her closer and buried his lupine muzzle into the softness of her hair.

She took a deep breath and looked up, right into his face. He winced, not sure how she'd take his appearance. She barely batted an eyelid, her hands soft as she wound her fingers into the thick ruff on his cheeks.

"They were..." She couldn't complete her sentence, her full lower lip trembling as she looked around. Her face paled again as she looked around the scattered remains. Fear struck his heart as she flinched and looked away from the carnage, burying her face against his fur again. She thought he was a monster. How could she think anything else?

"I thought I was was going to die. That I'd never see you again. That I wouldn't get a chance to tell you—" She was talking again, her words muffled until she looked up, a soft flush on her cheeks. "I know it's probably a little early, but...I love you, Jack. Fur, claws and all."

His heart leaped, his anger draining away, leaving just relief and something else in its wake. Hope for the future, and love. Jack sighed as the emotion burst forth from his heart and swelled throughout his mutated body. He loved her so much the sun, moon and stars wouldn't be enough to prove it. She was his mate, the other half of his soul, the light to his darkness...he ran out of clichés and just held her.

She was his. She was safe. That was all Jack needed to know.

Chapter Twenty

Lillian couldn't stop the shivering. It pervaded every part of her body, right down to her damn fingernails. How pathetic was that? She wasn't even hurt, apart from the injury to her dignity. Still she clung to Jack, reveling in the feel of his soft fur and the strength under her hands. Absently, a part of her brain was still yammering away that she was stood, half naked, in the woods hugging an extra from *The Wolfman.* She ignored it.

The body holding her started to shift. The snick and pop reached her ears at the same time the fur she'd been holding retreated back under smooth, warm skin. It was the first time she'd been touching him as he changed. A small giggle escaped her lips as she flattened her hands over his chest.

"What?" He had a curious smile on his lips as soon as he reached human form. "What's so funny?"

Leaning in, she breathed his scent in deep, filling her lungs with the essence of him then rubbed her cheek against his chest like a cat. She'd know him anywhere, just from his smell. It wasn't that it was obvious, or bad, just unique to him.

"You vibrate when you change. All over your skin. It feels funny."

He laughed a rich sound of unhurried amusement and delight, as though they were a couple out on a date, rather than standing in the middle of a clearing in the forest surrounded by the remains of people who'd tried to kill them.

He was beautiful. She didn't have any other description for it as she looked up into his smiling face. The grin that curved his full lips and the sparkle in his deep blue eyes...just beautiful. Love surged through her in a steady stream, overflowing from her full heart.

"If I didn't know before, now I do." He bent his head to claim her lips, teasing her with soft brushes of his. "I love you."

I love you.

Those three little words wiped the slate clean. Her shivering stopped as she lifted on her toes for another kiss and then clung to him like a life raft in a stormy sea. She never wanted to let go, her entire body shaking so much her teeth rattled. The sound of someone clearing their throat made her lift her head. They were surrounded by the wolf pack.

"Fuck me, there's a foot up there."

Nic looked up with awe and amusement on her face. Lillian followed her gaze. Sure enough, nestled in the fork of a branch like a grisly Christmas decoration was a lone boot. Still laced up, the ragged edge of bone showed stark against the grays around it. Blood dripped drop by slow drop.

Suddenly, Lillian was very glad she didn't have the same sense of smell they did as the stench of the bodies washed over her. The smell of fresh meat and opened intestines. Stronger than smelling salts, guaranteed to make a girl lose her lunch, or kill her appetite if she hadn't managed to eat. If she were a vampire, she'd be fine. Plenty of blood around to snack on.

She gasped as she remembered Darce. How could she have forgotten? He was still out there somewhere with that Blood creature.

"Jack—"

He wasn't listening, his hand held up sharply for silence. Around them the wolves dropped silent, their bodies taut with tension and their faces intent as though they were listening for something. A frown creased her brow as she stilled. There, on the edge of hearing. A mechanical sound...

Thumpthumpthumpthump.

"Gunships!" Jack yelled as the first one came into view over the tree line. "Fur on, bug out!"

The group around her scattered. Without asking, Jack grabbed her and threw her over his shoulder as he changed. His shoulder went from human-broad to massive and furred in a heartbeat. She gasped and tangled her fingers in his soft fur. There was no thought of arguing her independence. Any pride disappeared as the gunships opened fire and the clearing once again became a battlefield.

Bullets slammed into the ground around them, explosions spewing dirt and worse into the air making them dodge. She screamed in terror and hung on for dear life.

Nic was three steps behind them, running low and fast to avoid becoming a target for the guns above. She looked like a goddess of war, covered in blood and her ice-blue eyes inhuman in the spotlights. Lillian stared as she took three running steps and launched herself into the air. Hands forward and her body a graceful arc, Lillian thought she was going to crash into one of the broad treetrunks they passed.

She didn't. Instead her body changed in mid-air. The human form collapsed in on itself and the wolf-woman exploded out of it like some kind of organic origami. Using the trunk as a springboard, she veered off to the left, howling a warning.

Bullets slammed into the trees as Jack sprinted through them, changing direction to follow Nic. The wolf-woman's slender figure wove and dodged through the trees, with the rest of the pack following her.

They were surrounded. Searchlights stabbed through the trees from all directions. The gunships hovered, trying to get a clear shot at them through the thick branches overhead. Shouts and yells accompanied smaller caliber bullets as they flew and zipped from everywhere. The wolves yipped and danced as though they were being harassed by hornets.

They were being herded somewhere. Panic filled Lillian's chest. She could see where this was going. They would herd the wolves into a clearing, a killing ground, and wipe them out. The fact that she'd be in the middle of the slaughter made no difference. Her encounter with the soldiers had made it clear that, if they got hold of her, she was a dead woman. But her heart ached for the wolves. They'd done nothing wrong, other than serve their country, and look where it had got them. Hunted down like dogs.

"Left, left!" she yelled, pointing at a gap through the trees as Jack swung around. Just beyond a small group of soldiers sat the distinct shape of troop vehicles. Armored Humvees painted black. Unbidden amusement swam up. Add some bling wheels and they wouldn't look out of place on the streets. But she wasn't interested in the wheels—she was interested in the heavy-duty gun mounted on the top of one.

The pack wheeled as one. Fear and terror showed in the eyes of the soldiers as the wolves broke away and ran the gauntlet instead of taking the easy option they were being herded toward. Lillian's lips quirked. Served them right for treating the wolves as dumb mutts when they were anything but.

Bullets meant nothing as the wolf pack slammed into the line with a ferocity that would leave survivors with nightmares for the rest of their lives. If there had been any. Within seconds, the wolves had rolled through, rendering living, breathing soldiers to bloodied remains.

"Nic, Sanders! Designated drivers!" Jack speed-shifted to human and yelled as the team swarmed through the gap they'd made in the human forces. Instantly the two wolves broke off and ran toward the trucks. By the time they reached the doors, they were both in human form. Hardy as their other forms were, paws were useless for driving.

"Richards, man the gun. I want those ships gone!"

As the sergeant vaulted into the back of the second vehicle, Jack wrenched the door to the first open and put Lillian down in the passenger seat as Nic fired it up.

"Stay," he ordered, cupping her cheek with a gentle hand. Covered in blood, she looked terrified, her eyes wide and dark. "It'll be okay. Nic will look after you."

He shut the door, encasing her in its bulletproof cocoon. She'd be safe now, and he could concentrate on what he needed to do without worrying about a stray bullet taking everything that mattered from him. He rejoined the battle, leaping into the open back of the troop carrier to grab an unsecured rifle.

The Humvees roared to life, careening out of the clearing and through the narrow forest roads. In the other vehicle, Richards had the machine gun up and running. The heavy weapon spat death and destruction at the gunships above them as the rest of the pack dealt with the human troops. Jack didn't spend too long looking. He had better things to do and, despite the fact that they were all easy with nudity, there was something about a guy firing a machine gun while butt-naked that was just *wrong.*

"Take that, you bastards!" Jack snarled, rifle tight into his shoulder as he took down soldier after soldier with the Project's own weapons. They died easy. The lucky ones. They'd get a full military funeral with honors. Their names would be remembered with pride.

They wouldn't be forced into a cage bed and infected, then used in experiments to satisfy scientific curiosity. They wouldn't end their days with a bullet to the back of the head and be buried in an unmarked grave.

The breakneck chase through the trees didn't last long. Richards was a man of many talents. Apart from his plumbing prowess, he was the best gunner among them. The big weapon danced under his hands, the bullets cutting through the air and branches alike, the former crashing down onto the men who tried to follow them.

The trees opened up, the air above them clear. Time slowed to a crawl as the gunships roared into view. A wordless war cry erupted from Richards' throat as he wrenched the machine gun around. Bullets tore the air, lighting it up like a fourth of July parade. They traced a delicate line toward the helicopters. Jack held his breath. They slammed into the side of the first gunship, tearing metal up as they sought the blade motors.

He had to hand it to Richards—the guy didn't waste time. No messing around trying to bust the bulletproof glass to get to the pilot for him. No, if he needed a chopper out the air, he simply removed its ability to remain airborne.

Two blades shredded on contact. The gunship groaned and listed to the side, like a fly with its wings pulled off. The other one was too close, couldn't move out the way quickly enough. The remaining blades on the crippled ship swung around, slicing through the metal of the second like a hot knife through butter. Both tumbled toward the ground, trashing trees as the troops in the back were flung clear like ragdolls.

Jack pounded on the roof behind him. "Incoming! Faster!"

The Humvee lurched under his feet as Nic put her foot down, the vehicle threatening to shake apart as she pushed it past its operational limits. She wouldn't. Nic was an excellent driver, always able to coax everything from whatever she drove. Clinging to the side of the turret like the rest of the pack, Jack didn't care even if she did trash the thing. It was a Project vehicle; he didn't have to worry about paying the bills. All he cared about was putting distance between them and the tumbling, rolling mass of fire and death bearing down on them.

Locked together the gunships crashed into the trees. Metal screamed. *Thump...thump...thump.* The second ships blades still rotated, trying to pull away from certain death, even with its cockpit shorn in two and blood decorating the inside of the windscreen.

The valiant effort was for nothing. The nose of the first ship kissed the ground and caught. It tumbled, taking its partner with it. Both rolled, metal folding and fire blossoming in a hypnotic dance. Jack held his breath as a blade came loose, cartwheeled, and missed the second pack vehicle by a hairbreadth. Then they were free, the roar of the Humvees's powerful engines carrying them into the darkness and to safety.

They escaped into the darkness of night. The powerful vehicles roared along the forest roads at breakneck speed, careening around corners and taking out smaller trees growing too close to the dirt tracks. Great. The Project wouldn't need a tracker to follow their trail—even a kid could draw them a map. Standing in the back of the first vehicle, Jack closed his eyes for a second and let the cool air wash over him as they climbed higher, past the foothills and into the mountains proper. They needed to ditch the vehicles, and fast.

Finally, he deemed they were clear enough and pounded on the cabin roof again. They'd taken down the gunships and stolen the Project's transport. For an hour or two, at least until those they'd left alive could summon backup from base, they were safe.

The vehicles pulled to a stop in the next clearing and the pack de-bused, lean, naked bodies leaping with inhuman grace from the armored vehicles to crowd around Jack.

"Everyone okay?"

He did a quick head count as Sanders slid out the cabin of the second vehicle. Instantly, the wolf's eyes searched the pack, hopping from one member to another until he found what he was looking for. Relief in his eyes as he spotted the tall form of Richards, skipping over the others. Jack sighed inwardly. That was a situation that needed sorting, and quickly.

"We're down one," Richards said bluntly, looking around.

Jack did a quick head count. "They must have Darce. He wasn't with Lillian when we found her. We—"

"Boss, we got a problem."

Jack waved his hand at the sound of Nic's voice behind him. "Hold one, Nic. Right, they have Darce, so we need to go b—"

"Boss! You reall—"

"Nic!" He all but roared in frustration, his voice sharp with worry for his second in command. "I'm dealing with some—"

"Lillian has been shot."

Three little words. Unlike those other three little words, these were ones no man wanted to hear in his lifetime. Not when applied to his mate, the woman he loved.

The ground surged beneath his feet, a great yawning chasm trying to swallow him up. He couldn't allow that. Gritting his teeth, he forced steel into his backbone and looked at his men anew.

"Richards, sort a recon. Two men. Find out where Darce is.

Don't let them see you, don't get caught. Everyone else, secure the perimeter."

The orders spilled from his lips automatically, his training taking over despite the fear clawing at his gut. Wheeling, he was around the Humvee in a heartbeat. He wrenched the door open. The smell of blood hit him. Old blood, mixed with dirt. Nic had to be wrong, if his mate had been shot, there would be fresh blood.

Lillian rested back against the seat, looking pale and still. Jack's heart plummeted from its sudden leap of hope. Too pale and still. Her chest barely moved, just the slightest flutter to indicate she was still alive.

"Sweetheart? You okay?"

He leaned in to brush his fingers over her cheeks. At his touch, her eyelids moved, lashes fluttering like dark crescents on her alabaster cheeks.

She opened her eyes and smiled. Jack's fear became crippling, slicing his insides to shreds while he was powerless to do anything about it. Her eyes held Death, and he was almost here.

"Hiya, handsome." Her voice was little more than a whisper. "Did we get clear?"

"Yeah. We're safe. Sweetheart...look at me," he ordered as her head fell to the side, her eyes beginning to close.

"Where are you hurt?"

He tried to soften his voice, but it still emerged as a bark, raspy with pain and worry. Her head rolled on the back of the seat as she tried to focus on him.

"Everywhere. My back. I can't feel my legs, Jack."

Panic rang in her voice as she tried to move. Her eyes widened, the whites clearly visible as she struggled against the seat. As she did, her back came away from the vinyl and the scent of blood and worse washed over him.

He swallowed, fighting back bile as he carried on stroking her cheek to get her to calm down. She was gut-shot. Which meant, out here, she was dead. Internal bleeding and the contents of her stomach or intestine would already be fouling her abdominal cavity.

"It's okay, sweetheart. When were you shot?"

He cast a glance at the door, looking for the bullet holes. There weren't any. She must have been shot when he was carrying her and he'd missed it under everything else when he'd put her in the car. A low moan welled up and tried to claw its way out of his throat. One he quickly swallowed to avoid panicking her further.

"Sweetheart, it's going to be okay. But I need to know…when were you shot? In the Humvee or before?"

She was panting, her breathing fast and light. He didn't need to test her pulse to know it would be fast and faint, fluttering like a tiny bird in a cage. Shock. She'd lost too much blood. Tears stabbed the back of his eyes like hot pokers as pain stole his breath.

"Please Jack, help me." She lifted her hand from where it rested on the seat. It was covered in fresh blood. Hers. "Please, I don't want to die."

Jack froze as he realized what she was saying. She clutched his arm, her fingers biting deep with the strength of the dying. Her dark eyes pleaded with him, tears spilling over her lashes.

"I can't, sweetheart. I wish to God I could, but—"

Her hand dropped, and his wolf howled in rage at his words. For the first time ever, the beast within raged against him, slamming against the bars of its confinement to be free.

Jack gritted his teeth and fought for control as it tried to break loose from its prison of flesh. He could read its intent: to get free and bite Lillian.

Even if she was bitten as her human heart beat its last, as soon as the LY16 virus was in her system, it would do its insidious work. Because she wasn't Project, she hadn't been vaccinated against infection. A bite wouldn't kill her like the guards...

"If you don't, I will." Nic's voice rang out, clear as a bell, from behind him. Jack whirled, his chest heaving, and glared at her.

"Like *fuck* you will. She doesn't know what she's asking. What kind of life she'll be letting herself in for."

"Bullshit!" The female wolf threw back, her eyes blazing with heat. "That's a cop-out, and you know it. If you don't, she doesn't have a life. Period. Get out of the way if you're too scared to do it."

"Stop it, just stop it." The weak voice from the cabin stopped both of them in their tracks. "Please Jack, I don't want to die alone."

Chapter Twenty-One

She didn't have long. Lillian could feel her strength ebbing away as cold dug its sharp fingers into her body. Shock and blood loss, her brain told her. An adult human only needed a thirty percent blood loss for some pretty serious problems to develop. Anything past that and the patient was in deep shit.

The wetness on the seat and dripping down into the foot well told Lillian she was well past the problem stage and high-tailing it over the deep shit horizon. She welcomed it. If nothing else, the cold numbed the agony that her abdomen had become.

Jack wheeled around at her words, pulling her into his arms. She went gratefully, craving his hotter-than-human body heat.

"Its okay, sweetheart, I'm here. I'll always be here."

The low rumble of his voice against her ear was a comfort. Tears coursed down her cheeks as she clung to him. Shivers racked her as her heart fought to pump blood that simply wasn't there anymore.

"You can't stay." Agony of a different sort raged through her. "They'll be coming for you. You have to go."

He shook his head, the violent movement jostling her. Unable to help herself, she mewled in pain. Hand threaded in her hair, he made her look him in the eye.

"I am *not* leaving."

A wave of anger washed away the lethargy that was trying to claim her body and drag her down into the depths, like a riptide waiting for the unwary.

"Don't you *fucking* dare!"

She shoved him away, incandescent with rage. She lashed out. The slap as her hand contacted his cheek rang out like a gunshot.

"What are you? Some sort of fucking martyr? Don't you *dare* use me that way. If you won't save me, then save yourself. Get out of here and take the fight back to them. Those people came to my hospital and tried to kill people. They tried to kill you. They killed me. And if you won't save me, you *will* avenge me. Or, by God, I'll fucking haunt you."

He looked at her. Then his lips quirked.

"How can you haunt me if I'm dead too?"

"I'll find a fucking way, believe me. Even if I have to drag your sorry ass back into the land of the living to do it!"

She watched as amusement warred with agony. She knew he considered himself an animal, something less than human. A mistake. Reaching out, she cupped the cheek she'd slapped.

"Jack. I love you. Whatever and whoever you are. I'll love you as long as I live, even if it's a few minutes here in the car, or until we both grow old living in the forest on four paws." Her voice was soft, her words heartfelt. "Love doesn't care about appearance. It cares about what's in here." She tapped the center of his chest. "Follow your heart. The heart of a good man. It will tell you what to do."

Tears streamed down her cheeks unabated. He nodded, his expression shuttered. All hope fled. He was going to let her die, bleed her last in the passenger seat of a stolen military vehicle, rather than turn her into the creature he was. No doubt they would bury her right here, an unmarked grave under the leaves. Would he visit her in the years to come? Or would he walk away and never look back?

He leaned in, his lips claiming hers in a last kiss. She wrapped one arm around him, the other flopping uselessly at her side. Her heart stuttered in her chest, pounding painfully to pump nothing. Pain gripped her—agonizing, all-encompassing pain—then started to fade away. She breathed out, and her lungs stilled in her chest.

She was dying. The darkness rose to claim her as Jack's scent wrapped itself around her. Sorrow filled her. She loved him so much, and she had lost him.

"I'm so sorry, baby," he whispered against lips that could barely feel his warmth.

Then he bit her.

Fire and pain dragged her from the cold depths she'd fallen into. Hard chains lashed out and wrapped around her body, as a thousand hooks stabbed into her cold flesh. She opened her mouth and screamed as they pulled her into unimaginable heat. Every cell in her being protested, turning her inside out as they tried to escape the agony.

Dimly, she was aware of being carried. She didn't care. Whatever they did to her was nothing compared to the torture of her own body. Acid raced through her empty veins, filling them with a fiery liquid that reached every part of her, arms, legs, feet and fingers. She gasped, her back arching so hard she felt each vertebrae break.

This was it, she was really going to die. Just as she'd seen the guards in the hospital die. In tormented anguished. Perhaps not all people could be changed. Perhaps Jack and the other wolves had been different to start with...

Her bones snapped and shifted, joints popped and changed configuration. Forcing her eyes open, she looked down. Her body wasn't her body anymore, but it wasn't wolf either. Her limbs shifted, changing shape as the skin melted and slithered over them as if it had a mind of its own. She screamed as her mouth changed shape, razor-sharp teeth erupting from her gums to fill the forming muzzle. Her scream altered tone, became a howl of pain and rage.

"Oh my God, I'm sorry, sweetheart."

Jack was at her side, trying to calm her down, his hands smoothing down her changing limbs. Heat replaced the agony in a never-ending cycle. She rolled to the side and vomited up the bile in her stomach until all she could do was dry-heave, that miserable feeling adding to the legion of torment.

"It'll be over soon, I promise. Then you'll be better than new."

On her hands and knees, watching her hands change from the delicate, finely boned pianist's hands her grandfather had always commented on to huge, brutish paws, Lillian held onto his words like a mantra. And, when her back arched again, the vertebrae re-breaking, she took them with her into the welcoming darkness.

Light. She hated sunlight in her eyes in the morning. Lillian grumbled under her breath and tried to pull the duvet up over her head. Her questing fingers searched for the edge but couldn't find it. Where had it gone? She patted down her body and then around it. Where was the damn duvet? She'd always been sensitive to the cold. So if she wasn't covered with the duvet, why was she so warm?

The sense something was wrong pulled her the rest of the

way out of sleep. Opening her eyes, she got a swift impression of swaying branches above her before the brightness forced her to squeeze her eyes shut. Was that the sun? If so, who had turned the brightness up by around a billion watts?

Cautiously she cracked one eyelid. Yup, those were branches above her. What was she doing in the middle of the woods? She cracked a second eyelid and searched her memory, but it remained stubbornly blank. Something was different, though, she knew that without the aid of memory.

Yeah, no shit Sherlock. You're in the middle of the woods, I'd say something's different, all right. She ignored the sarcastic little voice and rolled to her side. She ached, as if she'd broken every bone in her body.

"Ugh." Okay, she wouldn't try that again for a while.

Rolling to her feet, she swayed, fighting the dizziness that wanted to drop her back to the sleeping bag she'd been lying on. Confused, she ran a hand over the clothes she had on. Camouflage pants and a wife-beater. They weren't her clothes. They looked more like...

The wind changed direction, brushing the hair from her face. Her eyes snapped open. With the wind came something else. Something...amazing. She inhaled deeply. Everything smelled so *good.* Especially one scent that stood out from the rest. A smell so mouth-wateringly perfect she'd taken two steps in that direction before she realized what she was doing.

She stopped, jerking to a standstill as memory crashed back, washing over her like a storm driven tidal wave. There was no stopping it or slowing it. Before her eyes, the events of the last few days crammed into her head like a never-ending stream. From Jack being wheeled through the hospital doors blood-soaked and half-crazed to the agony after he'd bitten her, infecting her to save her life.

She was alive. Jubilation and awe coursed through her as she looked around with new eyes. With werewolf eyes. He'd done it—he'd turned her. Lillian dropped her head back and howled just for the pleasure of hearing the sound well up and rip from her throat.

"I'm alive." She giggled and spun in a circle, hugging her arms around her body over what she assumed were Nic's clothes. "Jack."

Taking a deep breath, she found his scent, the perfect one that made her want to drop to the ground and roll in it, and ran. The trees and the undergrowth faded to a blur as she passed, following his trail. She ran for the sheer hell of it, a celebration of love and life, her body strong and whole. She ran to find the man she loved, her mate.

She laughed as she ran, a light sound of delight. She could feel the energy in her body, a vitality she'd never felt before. Easily, she leaped over a fallen log, the lure of Jack's scent leading her ever onward. Finally she found him, slowing to a walk as the track petered out into a small clearing on the hillside.

Jack sat on a boulder, clad only in camouflage pants and his feet bare on the rock in front of him. His shoulders were hunched, a broad line that screamed despair and misery.

She took a step forward, wary now.

"Jack?"

He didn't turn, didn't look at her. Her heart stuttered. Something was wrong. Had he changed his mind…didn't he love her now that she was like him?

"They took Darce. We couldn't get to him in time."

His voice was low, arms folded over his knees as he looked out over the valley below. The words hit her, twisted something in her heart. Darce had sacrificed himself so she could get away. It wasn't something she intended to forget. She would fight to the last drop of blood in her veins to free him from the Project.

She took the last few steps to Jack's side. All she wanted to do was touch him. His scent called to her, more potent than any drug. She wanted to rub her body against every inch of his, mark him with her own scent so everyone would know he was hers.

"The others are out securing supplies. I stayed to watch over you until you woke."

"And now?" She folded her arms, preparing herself for the words she knew were coming. He didn't want her now. It had been a mistake.

"You're in your first month. You need to learn to control your change. Once you can do that, you can leave."

"Leave?" She couldn't help the tremor of pain in her voice. She'd been right, he realized he'd made a mistake.

He sighed and stood up, finally facing her for the first time since her conversion. Her gaze wandered over him, drinking in every detail of his appearance. Then she reached his eyes. Pain and fear filled them.

"You'll hate me. If you don't now, you will soon. I made you into an animal and there's no way to forgive something like that."

Love and understanding blossomed in her chest.

"I don't hate you, Jack. I never could. I never will. We'll get Darce back, I promise. All of us, together."

Smiling, she stepped forward and reached up to touch his cheek. "You and your men were made what you are in pain and fear. I was made what I am because of love. You gave me the gift of life."

She reached up on her tiptoes and brushed her lips over his. “Now let me give you yours back.”

About the Author

Born and raised in Middle Earth (otherwise known as the Midlands, England), Mina Carter has (fortunately) never been mistaken for a hobbit. After a slew of careers ranging from logistics to land surveying, she can now be found in the wilds of Leicestershire with her husband and young daughter.

Eternally curious, Mina never tires of learning new things, dabbling in weird and wonderful things such as aromatherapy, corsetry, chainmail-making, welding, canoeing, shooting and pole-clinging (closely related to pole-dancing but for those terrified of heights and allergic to hitting the floor) to name but a few.

A full time author and cover artist, Mina can usually be found hunched over a keyboard or graphics tablet, trying to get the images and words in her head out and onto the screen before they drive her mad. She's addicted to coffee and Nutella on toast.

E-mail: Mina@mina-carter.com

Website: http://mina-carter.com

Twitter: http://twitter.com/minacarter

Facebook: http://facebook.com/mina.carter

Facebook Page: http://facebook.com/minacarterauthor

The man who vows to protect her may be her biggest threat.

Savage Hunger

©2012 Shelli Stevens

Savage, Book 1

Being the daughter of a world-renowned scientist, Sienna Peters has struggled to carve out her own career in the field. But her world is sent spinning when she discovers a secret species being held in the lab where she works, and the horrible things being done to them. Compelled to do more than hand off an information-packed jump drive to her father, she sets out to free the creatures.

The minute his team enters the compound, federal agent Warrick Donovan knows their mission will have more trouble than they bargained on. Unfortunately, trouble comes in the form of Sienna Peters, the younger sister of his close friend. Now not only does he need to save her pretty ass, he needs to discover just how involved she is with the imprisonment of the shifters.

Sienna knows she should trust no one—not even the man she might still love. But as the danger escalates and past passion ignites, her heart has other ideas. Even when the shroud of mystery is ripped off more than one stunning truth...

Warning: Must love alpha males, be intrigued by federal agents who may or may not shift into wolves, and most importantly be prepared for intense action of the dangerous and sexual kind.

CPSIA information can be obtained at www.ICGtesting.com
Printed in the USA
BVOW07s1409211014

371723BV00003B/189/P

9 781619 212770